THE M STRAIN

BRADLEY MICHAEL

PART ONE

1

Donald was sitting on the couch in the den when the noise came. "What's that?" he asked his wife. Shelly responded with a grunt and a shake of her shoulders. The grinding was somewhat metallic in nature; more like metal being scraped on the street, being destroyed. They both jumped up and rushed to the front bay window in the living room. Outside the world was a dimming white. Earlier that day a small snowstorm had engulfed the small community in Southern Indiana. The snow plows were quick to get out and most of the streets were clear. Okay, fairly clear. The street that Donald and Shelly Taylor lived on had been cleaned until the asphalt was showing. Hey that's what they paid their homeowners dues for, right?

As Shelly grabbed one end of the curtains to peek through, Donald grabbed the other end and threw full open his side of the curtains. What they saw puzzled them. A car was driving quite fast through their neighborhood. Only the car wasn't exactly in good shape. As a matter of fact, the car was falling apart. The driver's side front and rear quarter panels had been dented in pretty good. The driver's side view mirror was barely hanging on for dear life. The trunk lid was up and bouncing wildly. The front bumper was hanging off and was obviously the cause of the metal on asphalt noise that Donald had heard earlier.

A quick glance down the street told the story of the destroyed car. Almost every car parked on the side of the street had been scraped, crashed into, or in some way damaged by the crazy motorist.

"Donald, look!" screamed Shelly. This sudden outburst snapped him back to the present situation and Donald realized that the motorist was still coming this way, swerving crazily and heading right for them. "Oh, shit!" exclaimed Donald as the motorist turned his car and headed right for the house. Donald and Shelly jumped back from the window. Shelly started a sprint towards the other room while Donald didn't make it two feet. His right big toe stubbed into the corner of the bookcase that housed their enormous collection of books. Donald went to the floor grabbing his throbbing toe and holding it in immense pain. What seemed like an eternity passed and Donald had wondered why the car never ran into the house. "Maybe it passed us," he muttered. Shelly finally returned to the room with a confused look on her face.

"Donald, what happened?" asked Shelly.

"I hit my damn toe on the bookcase and it hurts like hell!" snapped Donald.

"I meant with the car….are you okay honey?" asked Shelly.

Donald glared up at Shelly as she moved over to the bay window. Shelly drew back the curtain and her eyes went wide. She couldn't believe what she saw. Donald was still on the floor but recognized the look on her face. Something had happened. The car didn't pass them. Donald looked up and saw the steam from the radiator rising into the fading light of the day. He rose from the floor and hobbled over to the big, front, bay window. From here he saw now what Shelly was so surprised at. The car *had* careened towards the house. However, it was stopped by the massive oak tree that stood out in the front yard.

"I am glad that was there," whispered Shelly.

"You're telling me," said Donald.

"What do we do now?" asked Shelly.

"I guess we better see if the driver is okay," suggested Donald.

The Taylors hurried off to their bedroom upstairs to dress for the outside weather. Shelly fished through her top dresser drawer finding a pair of socks and then headed to the walk-in closet to grab her jacket. Donald grabbed his jacket off of the end of the bed; he had placed it there earlier after coming home from grocery shopping with Shelly. He then hurried over to his dresser and grabbed some socks. They both started down the stairs to put their shoes on and Donald stopped.

"I will meet you at the front door," Donald told Shelly.

"What do you mean meet me?" asked Shelly.

"I mean we don't know what state of mind the driver is in. I'm going to say the person is hurt but is he messed up on PCP or alcohol? We don't know. So I intend to bring some leverage. I'll meet you down there," stated Donald.

"Okay, well don't take too long," Shelly said with understanding eyes.

"I won't," assured Donald. "But keep the door locked until I get there, alright?"

Shelly started down the stairs and Donald walked back into the bedroom and headed for the walk-in closet. On his way he stopped at his dresser and opened the second drawer and fished around until he found what he was looking for. He approached the closet and reached in and flipped on the light and headed toward the rear of the closet.

He turned right, toward his clothes, and bent down. Donald pulled out a locked box. He shuffled the key he had just grabbed from his dresser and moved it from his palm into his fingers. He unlocked the box and grabbed his 9MM and a full clip. Donald inserted the clip and pulled back on the slide. A round was chambered and Donald was ready for whatever might happen. He made his way down the stairs and stopped by the kitchen on the way to the living room to put on his shoes. Shelly was waiting nervously by the front door when Donald came around the corner. Donald flashed the gun towards Shelly and she nodded ever so slightly. Donald left the safety off and then slid the gun between his pants and his lower back. He reached up and drew back the deadbolt and then unlocked the door from the doorknob.

The Taylors came out of the front door almost at the same time. The cold air pulled hard on their lungs and the slight wind that was there started almost immediately to nip at the skin beneath their clothing. Donald took a defensive posture. His right hand slid down the small of his back and he grasped the gun. He kept his eyes on the driver's side of the car and advanced in an arc towards the vehicle. Shelly hung back and stayed ever alert. As Donald approached the car he could see now that the driver's side window had been smashed. He noticed that the driver was a black male, maybe early thirties, with blood all over his face. As Donald got closer he noticed now that it wasn't only blood on his face; there were boils and sores that had formed on almost every inch of his disease-ridden mug. Donald realized that the blood on his face was not from the accident but from the boils and sores. He also realized that the gun was not going to be necessary. The driver was definitely dead. He slid the safety back on and pulled his shirt and jacket back over the piece. *Maybe the accident was caused because of his medical issue*, Donald thought.

"Donald, what's going on?" Donald's thoughts were interrupted by Shelly trying to find out what the hold-up was.

"Stay there, honey," Donald said. "As a matter-of-fact, could you go call 911? Make sure they bring an ambulance or something because this guy is not walking away."

Donald started to back away from the car when the sound of an approaching vehicle caught his attention. Donald looked up and saw a black van approaching. Shelly had already walked inside to call 911. Donald watched the van as it slowed in front of the accident. The back opened up and three large people jumped out dressed in white medical suits. The suits had their own supplied air from a small tank strapped to their back. Donald also noticed that two of the white-suited men were holding M-4's. The third had a Desert Eagle strapped to his leg.

"Who are you?" Donald shouted. The two men with M-4's, Donald could see through the face masks that they were men, headed straight for the driver's side of the wrecked car. The last man approached Donald.

"Sir, I am going to need you to come with us." said the man in the white suit as he tapped the gun at his side.

"Excuse me?!" exclaimed Donald.

"Sir, we have an issue we need to contain and I am going to need you to come with us."

"What is going on? What do you mean, *contain?*" asked Donald.

"Sir, is there anyone else in the house with you?" asked the man as he unstrapped his hulking gun holster.

"Well, yes my wife is but…" stammered Donald.

The man in the white suit spoke into his face mask, "We've got one inside, also." Another white suit man jumped out of the back and headed for the front door, M-4 over his shoulder. Donald was so surprised at the scene before him that he couldn't move and he didn't know what to do. Again Donald asked, "What do you mean *contain?*"

"Take your fucking hands off of me!" Shelly shouted as a man in a white suit shuffled her out the front door.

The man standing in front of Donald produced a badge and shoved it in Donald's face.

"Sir, we are with Homeland Security and I suggest you cooperate. This could go easy or hard for you both. It's your choice," the man said.

"Honey, they are with Homeland Security, just listen to them," Donald shouted over to Shelly after staring at the man's badge.

Shelly and Donald were escorted over to the van. At about that time two more black vans showed up and parked behind the first. Another man in a white suit exited the back of the second van and he had what looked to be a weird backpack on his shoulders. The two men that had been at the wrecked car shuffled past the first van with the body from the car. The two men threw the body into the back of the second van. At this time the white suit man that had initially approached Donald started pushing Donald and Shelly towards the last van. Donald peered over his shoulder and found out what the backpack was for. It was a flamethrower and the white suit man was laying waste to the wrecked car. It was completely engulfed in flames. The big oak the car had wrecked into was starting to catch fire also. Donald and Shelly were pushed into the back of the third van and the doors were slammed shut.

"Donald, what the hell is going on?" asked Shelly.

"I have no idea," said Donald. "One of the white suit men told me that they had an issue they had to *contain*." Donald used air quotes when he said *contain*. "Wouldn't there have been something on the news if there were some kind of outbreak or something?"

"Donald, I'm scared," said Shelly.

"So am I, honey. So am I."

EIGHT HOURS EARLIER:

Voyshaun was on his couch when the message came through his phone. "Damn it," he thought. He was in the middle of a new X-box game and he didn't want to be disturbed. He paused the game and reached for his cell phone. *New deal – HUGE! Want in?* it said. Of course he wanted in. Voyshaun had lost his job at the parts plant and was always looking for work even if it was sometimes a little illegal. Hey, a man had to eat. *Hell yes! When/Where?* he typed back. Voyshaun got up and headed to the refrigerator for a beer. This might take a minute. He made it to the refrigerator in time for the text to arrive at his phone. 'Wow that was quick,' he thought. He grabbed his beer anyway and returned to the living room. Voyshaun plopped down on the couch and grabbed his cell phone. *New location: OWD. Fell N 2 sumthing and have to deal immed… hour and a half.* Now that was quick. An hour and a half! This must be important, especially to deal down at the OWD, the Old Warehouse District. This just might be a big score, too. *I'm in,* he typed back. Voyshaun was suddenly overtaken by thoughts of what this new deal could be. *Couldn't be drugs, could it? I mean, that wouldn't be that quick.* Not only that but that kind of deal usually only happened at night. *Guns? Maybe so.* Again though, deals like that usually only happen at night. *And what does that mean 'fell n 2 sumthing'.* Voyshaun tried to push his questions aside. He would be finding out real soon. He got up and headed for his bedroom. Voyshaun turned on the hot water and let it run for a minute. He laid out his outfit for the deal; which included a gun holster. He had gotten that at a flea market downtown. He thought it was kind of cool. Once the water was hot enough Voyshaun adjusted the temp with the cold water and then jumped into the shower.

Voyshaun Mitchell was chomping at the bit when he pulled onto Credenza Street and headed east. The Old Warehouse District was coming up soon and he still had no idea what the meeting was all about. He reminded himself that it must be something really big to do the deal in the middle of the day. Voyshaun came to a red light and stopped. *Not much activity in this neighborhood anymore,* he thought. *It used to be booming with activity. Then the fucking dirty corporate bastards fired everyone and moved the business down to Mexico. Just like my job at the plant. What a rat hole.* His thoughts were interrupted by the light turning green and Voyshaun pushed on the accelerator. As Voyshaun started forward he looked up into the rearview mirror. He noticed someone was behind him. It wasn't that unusual, except for the fact of his location. Voyshaun's phone rang.

"Hello?" he said.

"Let 'em ahead of you and then follow 'em," said the voice.

"Darius? That you homey?"

"Course foo', follow 'em to the warehouse."

"Aight bruh," Voyshaun agreed.

Voyshaun slowed down and pulled to the right. The car pulled next to him and the driver locked eyes with him. The driver was of Asian descent, maybe Chinese, maybe Japanese. Voyshaun didn't know. Hell, they all look the same to him anyway. The driver was dressed in a nice suit with a thin, long, deep scarlet tie. He had a scar that went from the right corner of his mouth to the back of the lower lobe of his right ear. Voyshaun thought the driver's stare was the signal to follow because immediately afterward the car pulled away and took the lead. Voyshaun followed for another four miles and then the car turned left. Half a mile up the road the car turned right into one of the many abandoned old warehouse lots. *This is a bumpy lot,* thought Voyshaun as he pulled in behind the lead car and followed it around back, all the while trying to avoid the pocked places in the parking lot. As they pulled around Voyshaun noticed Darius's car and was a little relieved. The lead car pulled over to the right and parked. Voyshaun followed suit but parked across from the row where the lead car had parked; next to Darius' car on the left. Voyshaun got out and Darius met him at the warehouse's entry door.

"You packin'?" Darius asked.

"O' course bruh, I'm no foo'," Voyshaun said. "So what's this deal all 'bout?"

Darius hushed and Voyshaun noticed the Asian driver slide past them and head into the warehouse. A look of disgust crossed the Asian's face but Voyshaun wasn't sure. It had happened so quickly and then the driver was through the warehouse's entry door.

Darius started, "I came across something and we have to get rid of it. Big bucks though if we can. I pulled a small job the other day for some rich guy. Said he had some stuff stolen by some ragheads and he wanted it back. So I say it's gonna cost ya, right. And he says okay. He agrees to our fee and then he says I can keep whatever else I find. I'm like, no shit dumb ass. Like I would have told him I found anything else." Both Voyshaun and Darius chuckled as Darius pulled out a cigarette and lit it.

"So anyway, I break into this house, find this stupid briefcase he wants and I am almost out of there when I see this safe off in the corner. For some reason, it's calling to me and I have to have whatever is in there. I bend over to check out the safe and realize it is a Sampson 850. I mean, come on, a Sampson 850?" This time they laughed rather than chuckled.

"So there I am breaking into this safe and I found a shit load of things. Not only was there some cash in there but there was also some jewelry and a few guns."

"That's what we're here about, man, guns and jewelry?" interrupted Voyshaun.

"Hell no idiot, let me finish. So I also find this case with some vials of liquid in it. Have no idea what they are but hey, I'm robbing the place right, so I take them. A few days later the word is out on the streets about these vials. So I found a buyer and here we are."

"Who's the buyer?" asked Voyshaun.

"Some Chinese guy and he's willing to pay a lot. Here's the deal: I hired two more guys for this job. We may need them. That makes four of us in for the cut. The deal should be two million; $500,000 for each of us!"

"What? Are you fucking with me right now? This could set us up for life, man," exclaimed Voyshaun.

"I am fo' real bruh. Now the other two are in there waiting so let's get our asses in there and look alive," said Darius.

Both men turned and walked through the warehouse entry door. As soon as Voyshaun entered the warehouse he could see why Darius had hired two more guys. He was just hoping that two more guys would be enough. There was a gang of Asian men standing in nice trimmed suits off to the left. The whole gang versus only the four of them would not be a fair fight. Voyshaun hoped that the deal went down smoothly.

Voyshaun could see the vast expanse of the warehouse. It was as long as it was wide. Only one office area occupied the whole bottom floor and it looked more like a break room. Glass was broken and strung everywhere. There was a set of stairs off to the left of the break room that ran up two flights to a catwalk that ran the entire length of the warehouse. Two offices occupied the upstairs and that was it. It seemed that the corporate thugs took everything with them when they went to Mexico. There wasn't even any scrap metal lying around. Beyond the two standing groups of men were three very nice Cadillacs; obviously the Asians' rides. Voyshaun noticed something else; the Asians were strapped. All of them carried automatic weapons. Voyshaun and Darius headed off to the right to join their group.

"Are you all here now?" asked a very well groomed, short Asian man.

"Yeah," said Darius.

The very well groomed short man turned and nodded. The driver side door on the third Cadillac opened and a very tall Asian man stepped out. *I didn't know they came that tall,* thought Voyshaun. The very tall Asian man stepped back to the rear of the car and opened the door. A stout old man stepped out and put on his hat. He, too, was very well-groomed and had an apparent air about him. It was one of confidence and it was seen by his men as they all stared in anticipation of his arrival. His jacket was thrown over his shoulders by the third man behind him and his cane was lifted from the backseat of the car. Voyshaun noticed that when the man started over to the group that he did not limp when he walked. *I guess the cane is for looks,* thought Voyshaun. The man came into the middle of the two groups and stopped at the small table that was there.

"Mr. Darius, I am Mr. Hong. We spoke on the phone."

"Yeah, I recognize yo voice. Let's deal," said Darius.

"Patience, my dear friend, is a virtue," said Mr. Hong in a soft, confident voice.

"Well, I ain't yo friend and I want to get this over with," came back Darius.

"Very well then, show me the vials please," said Mr. Hong.

Darius turned to one of the hired help and took the gym bag from him. He opened it and took out a smaller case that was shiny and silver and set it on the table. He opened it and turned it around for the old man to see. The old man could see that there were four vials of various colors. The old man's mouth turned into a smile. It was a smile like a little boy's smile on Christmas day. The smile he gets when he opens the first present under the tree and it is the BB gun he always wanted. After that, there are no more gifts. He only wants that one.

"Very well, Mr. Darius, my end of the bargain," said the old man as he gestured towards the short, well-groomed man. The short man came forward with a briefcase and opened it. He then turned it around for Darius and his group to see. After the short man turned the money case around, he grabbed the vial case and retreated to the back of his group.

"$250,000 American as we agreed, Mr. Darius", said Mr. Hong.

Darius was immediately heated and snapped back at the old man.

"You said two million old man! Don't fuck with us! We want our money!" shouted Darius.

"You may want to take what you can get Mr. Darius, while the money is here," said Mr. Hong.

"What do you mean while the money is here? Fuck that! The deal is off!" said Darius.

"As you can see the deal is not off, Mr. Darius. My associate already has possession of the vials. The money is here and you have one last chance to take it," said Mr. Hong. Darius and his group then noticed what was happening. The Asian gang had started to take a defensive posture and started to walk around them in a circle. Before the circle was semi in shape Darius' group started backing off. Darius had grabbed the money in his left hand and was now reaching for his 9MM with his right hand. Voyshaun, as well as the other two, also started reaching for their weapons. Darius happened to notice an entry door behind them. This one was much larger than the first one they came through and must have been used to move small machinery or parts through. Darius and company were almost through the door when Darius yelled to the Asian gang.

"Fuck you, Mr. Hong!" Darius unloaded with his 9MM into the Asian crowd. The Asians wasted no time in firing back. Darius and company made it through the door and beat feet like the devil was on their tail. That entry door, now exit door, was halfway down the warehouse and it felt like to Voyshaun that their cars were miles away. Darius, Voyshaun, and the hired help occasionally turned and fired back at the warehouse but most of the time they had was spent running. As they approached the cars the gunfire ceased. Voyshaun felt something bite his neck. *I've been hit*, he thought. He reached up to his neck and felt something odd. It was feathers. He realized then what had happened. They had shot a dart at him! Who knows what it had in it? Voyshaun hurried to his car and the hired help jumped into Darius's car with him. The two cars roared as they were started and the tires threw rocks everywhere when the accelerators were hit. *This is too easy*, thought Voyshaun. Instantly behind him, Darius' car went up in flames. It was such a loud and concussive blast that Voyshaun's car was rocked to the side. Voyshaun pressed harder on the gas and the car lurched forward.

"What the hell was that?" asked Voyshaun out loud. As his car came up to the warehouse parking lot exit Voyshaun noticed in his rearview that someone was on the top of the warehouse. *That person must have shot a rocket at Darius' car*, thought Voyshaun. He noticed that the person on top of the warehouse took a knee and then it was nothing but smoke. Instantly Voyshaun yanked the steering wheel to the left and skidded out onto the road. The rocket nearly missed him as it flew into another old warehouse. The explosion was insane as it again rocked Voyshaun's car. The gas pedal wouldn't go down any further as Voyshaun was trying desperately to get out of the enemy's range of fire. Voyshaun made it to Credenza Street and barely slowed down as he yanked the steering wheel to the right and again put the pedal to the metal.

Back in the warehouse, Mr. Hong seemed pleased.

"Mr. Chen, did you hit him?" asked Mr. Hong.

"Yes sir, I did," replied Mr. Chen.

"Good, the one with the dart will never realize what is happening until it is too late. I am pleased that they got into separate cars. Excellent work with the money case, Mr. Zhou. That car never suspected the bomb. Mr. Li, nice work with the RPG launcher. Let's hope that keeps him on the run," said Mr. Hong.

"Go, talk to your people and spread the disease," snarled Mr. Hong to nobody.

"I want him watched from a distance," said Mr. Hong. "Report back to me as soon as you see something."

Mr. Hong walked back to his car. His gait showed not only his confidence but also revealed that this was not the man you wanted to mess with. The rear door was opened, his jacket was taken from him from behind, his cane was laid on the back seat and his hat was removed. When he was seated, the door was shut and his hat was laid in his lap. The Asian gang now retreated back into the cars. The cars were fired up and were driven out of the warehouse. Mr. Hong picked up his car phone. As he dialed he could not keep the smile from his face. Someone on the other end answered in Mandarin and Mr. Hong spoke. He hung up the phone and lit a cigarette.

"To the airport, driver," said Mr. Hong. "Yes, sir," was the response.

3

The Taylors were ushered from the van after about a seven-hour trip. With a few small stops, presumably for gas, they had reached whatever destination their driver intended. Before Donald stepped out, both he and his wife were given paper medical masks to put over their mouths and noses. As Donald stepped out of the van he tried to take in the view. He was being quickly pushed towards a large entry door that was down a few steps and not easily seen from a distance. His glance around the area showed him several things. At the front of the cul-de-sac that the van was parked in, there was a large, blue, glaring sign that indicated they were at the Centers for Disease Control and Prevention, the CDC, in Atlanta, Georgia. *Why are we at the CDC?* thought Donald. He also noticed that the area around the CDC seemed to be deathly quiet. No cars passed on the street and no one walked by. He looked ahead and saw that the door they were being ushered towards was being held open by someone who was dressed just like their captors, although, this person didn't sport an M-4 or a handgun at their side. A white medical suit seemed to be all the rage with these people. Looking into the mask of the person in front of him Donald could see that once again a male figure was encased in the white suit. This man's build was less than the others, however, even with his smaller build, the breathing tank on his back and shoulders allowed him to take up a lot of the entryway. Donald took his wife's hand and led the way through the door, allowing her to follow him closely. The man holding the door eyed them cautiously. The only white-suit to follow them through the door was the man with the Desert Eagle strapped to his leg. The man holding the door moved away and the heavy door slammed shut with a resounding *thunk*. An echo went through the hallway and Donald could feel Shelly's hand tense around his. He squeezed tighter with the hope of reassurance. The man that was holding the door took the lead and continued walking down the hallway away from the non-descript door.

Desert Eagle caught up with the man in the lead and engaged him in conversation. It was muted, from the suit hoods and from the quiet talk, so that their prisoners could not glean any information from it. A prisoner is exactly what Donald felt like. After being shuffled from their house, told practically nothing, held in the back of a van for about seven hours, and finally shoved into the confines of the CDC, the Taylors still knew no more than when they were startled by the wreck in their front yard. *Maybe this has to do with the dead driver?* Donald thought. He didn't look so well and the guy with the Desert Eagle said they had to "contain" the situation.

Shelly's hand tightened around her husband's hand as Desert Eagle broke away from the lead man and fell once again behind them. The long hallway they were currently being marched down suddenly came to a 'T'. Without missing a beat the lead man took a right and immediately they came to a closed set of doors. The Taylors almost ran into the lead man and Desert Eagle had to back them up a few feet. The lead man grabbed his badge from his right suit pocket and swiped it on the entry pad on the right side of the door. He entered his 5 digit PIN and the door on the right swung inward. The lead man quickly glanced at Desert Eagle, and with a small push to the backs of the Taylors, they once again continued down the seemingly never-ending hallway. As they continued on Donald noticed a few things. First off, he did not see anyone else except for the two men he was with. This seemed a little unusual to Donald, this being the CDC and all. Second of all, he noticed neither man wore a badge in this area. Although a badge was used to gain access to this area, it was not worn by the lead man and it was quickly put back into his pocket after he used it. This was probably so that neither he nor his wife could get a name of either of the men. Lastly, there seemed to be a lot of doors connected to this hallway, presumably rooms, and no one had gone in or out of any of them.

A long walk brought the small company to a little recess on the left side of the hallway. Once again Desert Eagle stopped the Taylors short of the lead man as he brought out his badge and swiped a pad near a set of elevators. The lead man used the same procedure to call the elevator as he had used to open the set of doors they had walked through. The elevator was either fast or already sitting on this floor because a *bing* brought the doors open right away. This elevator was bigger than a normal elevator and mirrored one you might see in a hospital. Those were slightly bigger as they were used with gurneys in mind. Donald wondered what the CDC would need a large elevator for. As they entered the elevator the lead man maintained his position by the elevator call numbers and Desert Eagle pushed the Taylors to the far corner, away from the lead man. The lead man waited until all four were in the elevator and he pushed the number 15. The car began to move and it was a feeling Donald was not expecting. The car was going down instead of up. Donald glanced at the numbers again and realized that the numbers were doubled. The numbers were split into two columns and were of two different colors, red and blue. One column was now obviously for going up, the red buttons, and one for going down, the blue buttons. The elevator car reached its destination very quickly and immediately the lead man stepped out.

Desert Eagle pushed the Taylors out and they once again followed the lead man. This time the walk was not as long. After passing three sets of doors on the right the lead man stopped at the fourth. Once again he had to swipe his badge and enter his PIN. The difference now was that Desert Eagle had to do the same. Desert Eagle moved forward around the Taylors and at the same time he grabbed his badge out of his suit pocket and performed the same procedure. During this time Desert Eagle never took his eyes off of the Taylors except to enter his PIN. He maintained his gun on them throughout the entirety of the procedure. Silently the set of doors opened and the Taylors were rushed inside. There were two rooms and they were pushed past the first room and towards the door of the second. It was quick but Donald could see that the first room contained equipment, mostly specialized and therefore not recognized by him. The second room's door took the badge of the lead man and unlocked. The lead man opened the door and Desert Eagle pushed the Taylors inside. The lead man quickly shut the door. Donald cringed when he saw what was inside the second room. He saw a bed in the middle of the room. A dresser was off to the far wall right next to another door that was open slightly. Donald could see past that door and recognized a toilet and part of a shower. The front wall of the room was not a wall at all. It was a very large window. Currently, Donald could not see out of the window and he assumed it was probably a one-way mirror. Shelly caught his eye as she started to fall to the floor. She was crying heavily now and he barely caught her as she slid down to her butt. She had gotten a good look at the room also and must have come up with the same conclusion that Donald did.

"We're not leaving here are we?" she asked.

Donald swallowed a large lump in his throat and managed to squeak out a response, "We need to find out what's going on."

———————

Agent Johns reached up to remove his hood and Dr. Boone grabbed his arm to stop him.

"Not yet, agent," Boone said. "Wait until the results come back from the ventilation monitors. I know you masked them and we had the ventilation on high but I want to see what the filter tests come back with."

Dr. Boone made his way over to the right-hand corner of the first room and sat down in a small rolling chair and began to type away on a keyboard set in front of a six-screen display setup. The screens held all of the data the doctor would need, right at his fingertips. This included wall-mounted cameras throughout the facility and cameras outside surrounding entry points into the building. Other data included statistical characteristics of the second room which currently housed the Taylors. Oxygen level and temperature of the room, as well as the potable water level of the holding tank and audio and visual recording of the occupants, were on hand at the push of a button. Dr. Boone could also access other features of the building, tied mostly to this level only, such as ventilation speeds and ventilation filter responses. Right now he was bringing up the data for the ventilation filters on this level and within room number one.

"Okay, well that confirms that," he said to Agent Johns. Agent Johns' eyes widened slightly.

"The rest of the building, including this room, is free of the virus," Dr. Boone said. "You can remove your hood and suit if you'd like. I didn't think it could spread through air transmission."

Both men started doffing their protective suits. Both hoods were removed almost at the same time. Agent Johns then gestured for the doctor to turn around. When he did, Johns turned off his oxygen tank. Then they both turned the other way and Boone shut off Johns' tank. Agent Johns removed his large pistol and set it on the table next to the computer that Boone was using. He completely removed his suit and then replaced the gun back at his side. Boone was finished removing his suit by the time Johns put his gun back on.

"So what's next?" asked Johns.

Boone answered quickly. "Well, now that we have them contained we can take a deep breath and slow down a bit. This is a deadly virus we are dealing with and I want to ensure we are tracking and studying it carefully. I guess the first thing we can do is feed them. You were on the road for seven hours. Then we can let them get some sleep. I will talk to them tomorrow and then we can go from there."

Johns nodded and turned to the wall closest to the door in which they came into this room. He pressed a button on a call station next to the door and when someone picked up he spoke with authority.

"Yes, this is Agent Johns in room 15-04. Please bring down two meals and two empty cups. The hallway and room have been verified to be clean so please bring down the items as soon as possible. Thanks."

Dr. Boone was watching him and nodded his head when Johns turned back towards him. Boone resumed his work on the computer.

Fifteen minutes later there was a buzz at the door. Johns stood to answer. He opened the door and took both meals from the delivery person. On each tray was an empty cup for both of the Taylors. Johns walked both trays over to the door in which he shoved the Taylors through and at the same time Boone pressed a button on his keyboard. A small door within the main door opened and Johns shoved both trays through the small door. As the door was shutting he thought he heard shouting.

———————◆———————

At least thirty minutes had passed since they were put into this room. Donald was now sitting in the bathroom, at the toilet, with his wife. She was so worked up that she started getting sick. Luckily she was able to make it to the toilet in time. After she threw up, they sat there and barely talked. Shelly still sobbed slightly but mostly they both felt exhausted. A million thoughts ran through Donald's brain. The one that was at the forefront was why they didn't pat either of them down. Still sitting on the floor, Donald shifted slightly and felt the gun press into the small of his back. Now all he had to do was wait for the right time.

While wondering what they were going to do next, Donald thought he heard a metallic scraping noise in the direction of the doorway. His head, filled with thoughts and very sluggish, moved towards the bathroom door and he looked out towards the entry door. There he saw two plates of food being pushed through a much smaller door that was fit inside the larger one.

"Hey! What the fuck is going on?" he yelled. Quickly the door shut and it was as if the smaller door no longer existed. It was quite seamless, at least from this distance, and Donald started to stir to see what was laid out for them. Shelly, scared she was going to lose him, grabbed him and held tight.

"Come on honey, let's get you to bed," Donald said lovingly. He helped Shelly stand up and they both moved out of the bathroom and towards the king size bed in the middle of the room. Shelly was so out of it she did not see what had been laid at the door. Donald laid her head down on the pillow and then pulled the comforter that was on the bed half over her. He then patted her back and stood and moved towards the main door. There, on the ground, on silver trays, was exactly what he thought it was. Two trays full of food, one for each of them, and two empty cups. He grabbed both trays and walked back over to the bed. His wife had not drifted off to sleep yet and he touched her leg lightly.

"Shelly, honey? Are you hungry?"

Shelly's eyes opened slightly and her mouthed moved as if she was going to say something. Instead, she sat straight up and eyed the trays.

"Donald, I am hungry but what is to say that we should eat this?" Shelly questioned.

Donald eyed her and eyed the trays too. Finally, he spoke.

"I don't think there is anything wrong with this food. Two things jump to my mind right away as to why it should be okay to eat. First, if they wanted us dead they could have done it back at our house when no one was around. They could have just blamed it on the accident in our front yard and called it good. Second, we are at the CDC and from what I understand of the Center they are out to help people and not poison them. But, we should decide together. What do you think?"

Shelly eyed the trays and then her husband. She could eat something especially after her episode in the bathroom. Her stomach grumbled and she made a decision.

"I agree with you. They could have just killed us earlier if they wanted us dead. Okay, let's eat. Hand me one of the trays please."

Donald handed Shelly one of the trays and the empty cup fell from it and landed on the bed. Shelly grabbed the cup and eyed it questioningly. Donald shrugged and looked around. He got up, both cups in hand, and headed towards the bathroom. The sink in the bathroom was big enough to fit a cup underneath and he commenced to filling both cups with water. When he was done he walked back to the bed and handed one cup to Shelly. She had already started her meal and was devouring it ravenously. She looked up at Donald and shrugged with a small smile on her face. They both chuckled slightly and then continued their meal.

The personal jet that left O'Hare International Airport was about two hours away from landing in Paris, France when its passenger received a sat-phone call.

"Sir, we have a small problem with the package," said the caller.

"Tell me," said Mr. Hong.

"Well sir, the package is about eight hours away from its original location and there are two problems. The first problem is that the package is DOA, which is good, but it did not come in contact with anyone. The second problem is that the authorities have arrived and are disposing of the package and cleaning up the area."

Mr. Hong narrowed his eyes as if he was looking right through the cabin of the jet. He let out a small sigh and spoke softly.

"I guess the product is not transmittable through the air as we first suspected. This is a problem but this was only the first test. This, in a way, is good news. At least we know where to start on the second test."

The caller responded, "Yes sir."

Mr. Hong finished his thought. "You did well. You have maintained your honor. I will contact you in the future if anything else arises."

Before the caller could respond, Mr. Hong hung up the phone.

A smile crept onto his face and Mr. Hong beckoned the flight attendant over. Of course, this attendant came with the jet and worked personally for Mr. Hong. She was about 5' 5" with neatly cropped brown hair and a very short skirt. She had a Mid-Eastern look and she was very beautiful.

"Yes sir, what can I get for you?" she asked.

"Surprise me. Make it something hard though," said Mr. Hong.

With a very big smile and a small bow, the flight attendant walked off. *Business is going to be good*, thought Mr. Hong.

The jet was getting closer to Charles De Gaulle Airport in Paris, France and had already started its descent. A quick layover for fuel and then it was off to China. Another ten-hour flight would put the jet in Beijing. There the vials would be put to good use and Mr. Hong would personally see to it that the testing results would yield exactly what his benefactors were looking for. After taking a huge leap into the world of cyber-terrorism, and ultimately coming out ahead, his benefactors decided that they would reach into the world of bio-warfare. Mr. Hong had been given high responsibility during the cyber affair and had succeeded. Thus, the benefactors immediately placed him in charge of this new bio-warfare endeavor.

As the jet's landing gear extended, Mr. Hong produced a very large smile and clasped his hands together tightly. He was about to succeed in a way that his benefactors only had on their dream list. His mind ran wild and rampant with the thoughts of where they would place him next. However, after this foray, there was only one place for him: as a partner within the company. Normally it took more than two successful missions to move into a highly coveted spot. The immense ingenuity and intelligence, however, that was needed to pull off both of his assigned missions successfully were more than anything anyone had done before. Mr. Hong felt the jet land and quickly slow to a crawl. He unbuckled his seatbelt and was out of his seat when the jet began its taxi to the gate. The jet lurched to a stop slightly before the gate and Mr. Hong had to grab the seat in front of him to arrest his fall. Suddenly, in the cockpit, there was noise. The noise was odd and at a low decibel. Hr. Hong barely heard it. Suddenly a *thump* came from the cockpit and now Mr. Hong frowned. *What was going on in the cockpit?* thought Mr. Hong.

"Excuse me?" Mr. Hong looked around for the flight attendant and did not see her. Suddenly the bathroom door slid open and the flight attendant came out. She was no longer dressed in her short skirt. She had on a pair of jeans and a leather jacket. The jacket was zipped up halfway but Mr. Hong saw some sort of necklace dangling against her chest. Her hair was still cropped close and she had her right hand behind her back.

"Excuse me? Do you know what is going on in the cockpit? Why hasn't the door been opened yet? I would like to walk a bit in the concourse while we are refueling." Mr. Hong spoke directly to the flight attendant. However, it was as if she wasn't even listening. She continued towards him and when she was five feet from him she pulled her right hand away from her back. In it, she had a gun. She fired quickly, without saying a word, and watched Mr. Hong fall to the seat he was just sitting in. The shot was a perfect one and landed between the eyes of Mr. Hong. The gun had a suppressor and therefore was not loud. A small *pfft* was all the gun produced and then the job was done. As if on cue the cockpit door opened and the co-pilot stepped out. He was a taller man, about 5' 11", Mid-Eastern descent with short hair and a small beard. He looked at the flight attendant.

"Good job, now grab the case," the co-pilot said. The flight attendant nodded and turned to the left side of the jet. She opened the baggage carrier door and produced a small, silver, shiny case. The co-pilot stuck his hand out and the flight attendant handed him the case. He took it and gestured towards the door. The flight attendant immediately moved and unlocked the door. She swung the handle to the right and pushed open the door. The door swung open and the stairs built into the door were ready to use. Smiling, the co-pilot took the lead and the flight attendant followed. They stayed outside and walked to the tarmac to the gate next to theirs. Idling, ready for take-off, was another personal jet. They came to the door and it was open with the same set of built-in stairs. They entered the jet and upon entering they both walked towards the back. In one of the back seats was a man, their boss. The co-pilot handed his boss the case and then proceeded to the cabin where he made preparations to leave. The flight attendant immediately addressed her boss in Farsi.

"Sir, is there anything I can get you before we take off?"

Her boss replied, both eyes on the case. "Not now. Praise Allah."

5

Dr. Boone and Agent Johns showed up to work at about the same time. It was early, 0600, and the sun was just coming up.

"How did you sleep last night?" asked Dr. Boone.

"Not too bad," responded Agent Johns. "You know I exercise before I come to work so that helps." Dr. Boone shook his head in understanding.

Both gentlemen walked to the entry door that just the day before had been used to usher two individuals through and into captivity. Well, captivity sounded bad. After all, they were doing this for the Taylors as much as for anyone else. Whether the Taylors wanted to believe it or not it really was a quarantine. Of course, they still did not know yet what was going on. After giving them two trays of food, Dr. Boone and Agent Johns left for the rest of the night. The plan was to talk to them this morning after they had eaten and rested.

Dr. Boone swiped his badge at the entry door, entered his PIN, heard a buzz, and then opened the door. Agent Johns followed him in. Both walked to the second set of doors and Dr. Boone swiped his badge again followed by his PIN. Another buzz allowed them access and they walked to the elevators down the hall. Although it was 0600, there were some people roaming the halls. Mostly the overnight workers such as the cooks and janitors but there were a few agents and doctors walking here and there.

Dr. Boone called the elevator and when it arrived both men stepped in.

"Do you think they will know anything?" asked Johns. The question must have interrupted something Boone was thinking about because he suddenly looked surprised. The question finally registered and Boone answered.

"I'll be honest Agent Johns, I don't know. I will say they looked genuinely surprised last night and I can almost guarantee they will be pissed this morning."

Johns pursed his lips slightly, shook his head slowly, and drew out his only word, "Yeah…"

Agent Johns stood by the door to the holding and testing room while, once again, Dr. Boone swiped his badge and entered his PIN. The door made a small buzz and both men entered. As Boone made his way over to the computer desk, Johns immediately called in breakfast for the Taylors. Boone continued to fidget with the computer system bringing up possible windows that might be needed for what was coming next. Another fifteen minutes had passed and a sharp buzz jolted Johns' attention. He made his way over to the door and answered it. The breakfast for the Taylors had arrived and the cooks had included a smaller tray for the two men who were hard at work. Boone glanced at Johns and Johns nodded slightly. Boone pressed a button on one of the windows he had up and ready to use and the small door contained inside the larger entry door to the second room slid open. Johns hurriedly placed both of the trays designated for the Taylors on the floor and pushed them both inside. He stepped away and Boone pressed another button that caused the door to slide down.

Johns walked over to Boone as he was just finishing the screen setup for the upcoming event. All six screens were now filled with possible windows that might need to be used or monitored. One screen contained the windows that would monitor the environment inside the Taylor's room. Another screen held the windows that contained parameters about the level they were on. Yet another screen contained windows that could be used in helping with sedation of the individuals in the second room; if it were needed. Not all of the screens were full of buttons, data, or information. One screen was totally empty. Dr. Boone liked having one screen empty so he could quickly use that screen for anything that might come up. Having open screen real estate was always a blessing when the unthinkable happened.

"Well, I hate to do it but let's wake them up," said Boone. He touched one of the screens containing a control slider. The slider was marked in even increments and these increments were doled out in percentages. He moved the slider all the way to 100% and then touched a button that was identified as 'two-way'. The front of the glass wall that lined both rooms suddenly went from opaque to transparent. Both parties could now see each other.

As an afterthought, Boone said, "Plus, you just put their breakfast in there and I wouldn't want them to have a cold breakfast."

Johns nodded and said, "Hit it." Boone touched another screen and pointed at Johns. Johns slowly grabbed the microphone that was next to the computer and began quietly talking.

"Hello? Hello? Can you hear me?"

Donald and Shelly fell quickly asleep after eating what had been provided for them. They wrapped themselves up in the sheets and comforter and moved closer to hold one another. They did this mostly
because they were still scared and confused about what was going on.
Once Donald fell asleep the bad dream seemed to take hold of him
quickly. He dreamed he was back on the farm where he grew up in
Illinois. He was playing out in the fields with some of the kids that
lived in his neighborhood. For a country boy, the neighborhood happened to be quite large as most houses were not very near to each
other. Most of the kids were teasing and messing around with each
other knowing it was all in good fun. Someone mentioned something
about getting some sort of game going. When all of the ideas were
said the last kid that talked was someone that Donald did not know.
That was odd for him because he knew everyone in his neighborhood.
The new kid did look familiar like Donald had seen him somewhere,
but he was sure he did not live in the neighborhood.

The new kid said that they should play Truth or Dare. Every
one of the kids started laughing because they knew what the game
was. It always riled up someone because Truth would come up and
no one ever liked answering the questions truthfully. Finally, it was
decided that that was the game they were going to play. Somehow
Donald was picked to go first and, not wanting to be embarrassed by
some truth that he may have to tell, he picked dare. The new kid was
the first to speak and he dared Donald to touch the electric fence that
surrounded the field next to where they were hanging out. Living on a
farm, Donald knew better than to touch the electrified fences. Cows,
horses and other farm animals were kept in their pens because of these
fences and Donald had seen what the shock did to the animals when
they got too close. Donald was close to not doing the dare when he
looked around. Every kid was surrounding him and staring him down.

Their little intense faces were pleading with him to do it like it was something that they needed to see. Donald, as a little kid, quickly gave into the dare. Donald, as an adult, seemed to be hovering over himself watching what was about to happen and unable to stop it. Donald the kid walked over to the fence and stopped. He turned around and saw that every kid had followed him and was intently waiting. Donald turned back around and slowly started to touch the fence. When he got within a half-inch of the fence a bolt of electricity shot out and traveled down his finger, and then down his arm and to the rest of his body. The shock knocked Donald back about ten feet. Donald the watching adult knew that that would be impossible at that voltage. Suddenly, Donald the adult was thrown into the body of Donald the kid. He lay on the ground looking up at the sky. His view suddenly filled with all of the kids. All of their mouths were agape and all of their eyes were wide. The new kid pushed in closer and said, "Hello? Hello? Can you hear me?"

Donald woke with a start and sat up in bed. His body was soaked with sweat and the spot on the bed that he was just lying in was worse. He looked over at Shelly and she was still fast asleep. Donald shook his head trying to break away from the bad dream. As his head came forward Donald noticed two men sitting out in the next room.

"Can you hear me?" one of the men said.

Donald stared at them. It took a minute to wake up but he realized that he recognized both of them. The man asking the question was the one that had picked them up at their house the day before. The other man was the one that led them through the hallways of the CDC. That last thought had hit Donald somewhat hard. He had temporarily forgotten where he was. Seeing both men brought back anger and frustration. Donald nodded slowly.

"Good," said Johns. "If you want to wake up your wife, I have set breakfast over by the door. I recommend you get up and eat. The next few days are going to be hard and you will definitely need your strength."

Johns pointed over in the direction of the door. Donald's head turned slightly and he could see that there were two trays, sans cups, over by the door. Donald looked back at his wife and grabbed her shoulder gently. He shook it and she stirred. Slowly she rolled over in his direction and tried to cuddle next to him. She reached out to try to put her arm around him and she realized that he was sitting up. She opened her eyes slightly and the previous day suddenly hit her. She sat up quickly and pulled in closer to Donald. He hugged her tightly and spoke softly in her ear.

"Yes, we are still here. It wasn't a dream. They brought us breakfast and recommend we eat."

Shelly looked up at him and nodded. Donald kissed her forehead and pulled himself out from the bed covers. He walked over to the trays, picked them up, and walked back over to the bed. He handed her one and set his on the bed. He walked to her side of the bed, grabbed both of the cups that had been set on the floor the night before, and made his way to the bathroom. He filled both cups three-quarters of the way full and walked back over to the bed. He handed her one and set his back down on the floor. He then turned back around and went back to the bathroom to relieve himself. It was a few moments before he returned. When he did, he grabbed his cup of water and went to his side of the bed. They both were still eating when one of the men spoke again.

"Is it good?" he asked.

Donald stared for a moment and nodded affirmatively.

"Good. They do make some pretty mean grub here," he responded. "My name is Agent Johns and this is Dr. Boone. Do you know why you are here?"

Both of the Taylors stopped eating. They both stared through the wall glass and both nodded negatively. Johns sighed. He tried not to make it noticeable. Johns looked over at Boone. He nodded and Johns continued.

"We believe there has been the release of a deadly virus and that the both of you may have come into contact with it."

Both of the Taylors dropped their forks. Suddenly their appetite was not very high on their list.

Johns continued. "Yesterday, the car that crashed into your front yard may have been carrying the virus. More specifically, the driver."

Donald could easily recall what the driver looked like. Knowing now that a deadly virus may have been the cause made a lot more sense.

"You are here because we need to see if you contracted the virus. If so, we are going to find out what can we do to stop and isolate the virus from spreading," said Johns. "We have some information about the virus but not a lot. We need your full cooperation to attack this issue head-on."

Donald rose from the bed and approached the glass wall.

"Why should we help?" asked Donald. "You took us from our home without telling us what was really going on. You threw us in some kind of isolation and quarantine room and then you basically just leave. What part of any of that makes us want to cooperate?"

By now Shelly had joined her husband, and although she was scared, was trying to put on a face of determination and anger.

"You do understand what I am telling you, right Mr. Taylor?" asked Johns. "I am saying you may have contracted a virus and I want to help. You don't want to die, do you?"

Donald snorted in derision. "This isn't really about us, is it?" asked Donald. "What is it that you really want that helping us would help you?"

Johns took a deep breath and spoke. "Like I said we know very little about the virus but what we do know could possibly be very bad to a lot of people if what our Intel guys tell us is true. And by 'a lot of people,' I mean possibly everyone on Earth!"

Donald stood at the glass for a minute and tried to take in what Johns had just told them. He looked at his wife and then looked back at Johns. A quick glance over at the doctor showed that he was staring right back at Donald. They were either waiting for him to respond or for him to soak up the news. He needed time for both. He turned slowly and headed back to the bed, his wife in tow. They both sat at the foot of the bed looking at each other.

"What do you think?" Donald asked Shelly.

Shelly took a deep breath before she answered. "Do you think they are telling the truth?" she asked.

"They could be," Donald answered. "I can't think of any other reason why they would basically kidnap us and then throw us down here in this room."

Donald looked over at both of the men outside of the room and they were staring intently at the Taylors.

"If it got worse for some reason we would still have the…" Shelly spurted out. Donald stopped her quickly with a brush of his hand against her lips. He nodded in understanding and Shelly knew not to say anything more. Donald started talking again.

"So it looks like the only option we have is to cooperate. I am sure they could do whatever they want to us anyway, why not help make the process a little gentler? Plus, if we did contract something from that driver then I don't want to die like he did." Shelly nodded softly.

Donald, now on the same page as his wife, nodded back and then stood up. He walked over to the glass and started speaking.

"Okay, we'll cooperate. But we have conditions. We want to be a part of the information that you find out about us. We don't want to be left in the dark while you poke and prod and then we suddenly die. We'll cooperate if you just let us know what is going on," Donald bravely demanded.

Johns turned sideways from the glass and faced the doctor. They talked for a minute and they must have shut off the microphone because neither Donald nor Shelly could hear them. Donald was close enough, however, to glean some words from their lips. It seemed positive but without getting the full conversation the words could be taken out of context. After nodding a few times to each other, Johns turned back towards the glass.

"After speaking with the doctor, we can partially meet your demands. We can only partially meet them because of national security but..." Johns started. Donald interrupted immediately.

"National security? We're stuck in a fucking room in the basement of the CDC! What threat do we pose to national security?"

"...but," continued Johns despite the interruption, "We can keep you informed of the biological aspect of what is going on with you or, for that matter, not going on with you. The good doctor can do that part of it and I will attempt to give you as much information as I can.

Understand I will NOT tell you anything unless it applies to what we are doing right here, right now."

Donald fumed. His face became a little redder and his hands made their way to his hips. Standing there looking like an upset parent, Donald took a deep breath.

"Fine," Donald said. "But we want to know as much as possible. The minute I feel we aren't getting the information we should be, we're done with helping."

"Agreed," said Johns. He let go of the microphone and turned to Boone.

Boone touched his computer screens and cut the microphone. As he did his eyes flicked back and forth at the presented data.

"Well?" asked Johns.

Boone took a moment more touching his screens. Finally, he looked up at Johns.

"I'm not getting too much. He definitely got mad at your comment about not telling him everything. But based off of temperature, eye movement, and speech pattern, I don't see anything that would indicate he is lying. He is definitely telling the truth about them cooperating but he is also telling the truth about them not cooperating if we try to play them. I would be careful, Agent Johns, about leaving out too much information. I think we should start immediately with tests before they change their mind."

Johns nodded affirmatively and went back to the microphone. He waited until Boone had turned it on and then he started speaking.

"Mr. and Mrs. Taylor, the first thing we are going to have to do is take a sample of blood. I am sure you expected something like this to be on the docket and so it should come as no surprise. What is going to happen is that Dr. Boone is going to suit up and come into your room. He is just coming in for a blood sample from both of you and therefore is not expecting any trouble. Please remember the deal we made and cooperate."

Both Shelly and Donald slowly nodded their heads. Johns smiled slightly and let go of the microphone. He turned to Boone again and Boone turned off the microphone.

"Show me," Johns said. Boone brought up a window and put it on the upper left screen.

"All you have to do is press here and the gas will activate," said Boone. "I will have my suit on but even if somehow my hood comes off you still need to press this button to activate the gas. Neither they nor I will be harmed as it will just knock us out. As a matter-of-fact, it will knock us out quite quickly. If you have to enter the room to get me, there are two ways that can do that. You will have time to do what you need to as the gas lasts for several hours. The first way is to don your suit and then come in and get me. The other way, and the one I prefer because it saves us from any gas escaping out into this room, is to press this button right here. This button will turn the exhaust fans, which are always running, immediately to what is called 'emergency-run'. This will cause the exhaust fans to run up to 100% and pull all of the gas out of the room quickly. Then, come in and get me. Any questions?"

Johns shook his head no. Boone still wanted to make sure.

"You remember which button opens the door, right?" Boone asked.

Again, Johns shook his head yes. Boone stared at Johns for another moment and then sighed quietly. Boone stood up and walked over to the two-locker set that was against the left side wall. He opened the locker on the left and began pulling out his white suit. He grabbed every piece of the suit out of the locker and brought them over to the computer desk and sat down. Then he began donning the suit. Before he put on his hood he walked back over to the locker set and pulled out a small, smooth, silver case from the top of the locker where he got his suit from. He brought the case over to the computer desk and opened it. Inside, to the left, he found two, brand new needles with their associated vials stuck into a soft mold designed to carry and handle the vials without breaking. Off to the right, there were some cotton balls, a piece of long rubber that would be used to put around the arm, a few Band-Aids, a pair of gloves, and a small bottle of alcohol. Satisfied, Boone donned his hood, the final piece of his suit, and with the silver case in his hand, he headed over to the door that led to the second room

When Boone made it to the door, he nodded to Johns and Johns pressed the button that would open the door. The door buzzed and Boone proceeded into the second room. When he entered he noticed that the Taylors were sitting on the edge of the bed and it looked like they were calm and were going to cooperate. Boone continued into the room and he heard the door shut behind him. *At least Johns remembered that*, thought Boone. As he got closer to the Taylors, Boone stuck up his free hand in a placating gesture.

"I have the equipment necessary to take the blood sample," said Boone holding up the case. "Who would like to go first?"

Shelly raised her hand about halfway up. Boone looked at her and then at Donald. Donald looked back at Boone and then shifted to the side of the bed with his wife. Boone sat down and began fumbling through the case. The first thing he grabbed was the set of gloves. He put them on. He then brought out the needle, still capped, and attached the vial to it. Then he brought out the bottle of alcohol and a cotton swab and set them on the bed. Next, he grabbed the rubber tie and gestured for Shelly to show him her arms. She did and Boone saw that the left arm had a very visible vein. He pointed to that arm and she dropped the other one. Boone tied the rubber around her arm, about halfway up her bicep, and gave her vein a small tap. The vein started to bulge from the pressure and Boone wiped down the area with the alcohol. Once sterilized, Boone took the needle, opened the cap, and pushed it into Shelly's arm. She winced slightly but, for the most part, sat very still. As Shelly's heart pumped, the vial slowly filled with her blood. When it was filled, Boone took the needle out. He grabbed a cotton ball from the case and put it on Shelly's arm.

"Hold pressure here please," Boone said and pointed at the cotton ball. Shelly did so and Boone took the needle, capped it, and put it back in the foam holder within the case. He then grabbed a Band-Aid and put it on Shelly's arm over the cotton ball.

"Okay, your turn Mr. Taylor."

Donald moved to the spot where Shelly had just left and immediately held out both arms. On him, Boone could see that the right arm had the largest vein. Boone once again performed the same procedure that he had on Shelly. Afterward, he put a Band-Aid on the cotton ball, gathered his materials, took off the gloves, put everything in the case, and then closed it.

Boone looked at both of the Taylors before he stood up. They looked morose as well as scared and Boone wanted to reassure them.

"Mr. and Mrs. Taylor, I promise I will do everything I can to see that you are kept healthy and alive. I will let you in on as much as I can when I find out the information."

Donald grinned slightly and said, "Thank you."

Boone nodded and stood up. He made his way to the door and when he got there he gestured to Johns. Johns looked through the glass towards the Taylors. They were still sitting on the bed but now they were hugging each other. He looked back at the computer screen and touched the button that would open the door. A *buzz* sounded and then the door unlocked. Boone opened the door and went through. Johns ensured the door shut after the doctor came through. Boone walked over to the computer table once again and set the silver case down. He then walked over to where the lockers were and began doffing his suit. Once he was undressed Boone placed his suit in the basket next to the lockers. He walked back to the computer desk and reached for the silver case. Suddenly a phone rang. Johns jumped slightly and then shifted to answer it. He took the phone from his pocket and picked up. Boone stopped and listened.

"Hello?" Johns answered. After a small pause he said, "Right away, I'll be there in twenty minutes." Johns hung up the phone.

Boone was looking at him and Johns spoke up.

"That was the office. It seems they may have some info for me regarding this matter. I'm going to head to the office. Let me know if you find anything. Otherwise, I'll be back in a few hours."

Boone nodded and set the case back down. He touched the microphone activation button and pointed towards the microphone. Johns understood and stood up. He grabbed the microphone and started talking.

"Both the doctor and I have to go and start trying to find out what is going on. He is going to work with your blood and I need to get back to the office for a while. There might be some more information there." The Taylors stood and walked slowly to the glass. Johns continued.

"We are going to darken the glass again. I promise someone will be back with a lunch. In the meantime, try to rest if you can."

Boone touched the button that would darken the glass. He slid the control slide over slowly. He thought that it would be rude to just completely shut out the Taylors all at once. Instead of being rude, however, the act made him seem overly dramatic. The glass wall slowly faded away as the Taylors stood there looking at Agent Johns holding the microphone.

7

Dr. Boone and Agent Johns both made their way out of the room. Both men quietly made their way down the hallway towards the elevator. Boone was silently thinking about what would come from the blood results and Johns was thinking about what kind of information had been found. Both men, still silent, stepped into the elevator. Boone pushed the blue number 1 button and the elevator car rose. It traveled quickly and soon the doors opened. Both men stepped out and headed in opposite directions. Johns turned right and headed for the exit while Boone turned left and headed for the labs.

"I'll be back in a few hours," said Johns as he twisted his head towards Boone but continued walking. Boone acknowledged him by waving a hand in the air and he kept walking. Johns turned back around and was out the exit and headed towards his car within a few minutes. Boone once again came to a set of double doors a little further down the hallway and performed his normal entry procedure. A small buzz unlocked the doors. Boone disappeared through them lost in his own thoughts.

Johns drove his sleek, black car, obviously provided by Homeland Security, down Center Avenue towards the freeway that would get him to the other side of town and his office. The drive was about twenty minutes, sans heavy traffic, but Johns didn't mind. It was often that Johns tried to escape his work by just driving silently in his car. No music, no phone calls, and certainly no food. At least not during the times when he tried to wind down and relax. This job was often stressful and you had to find a way to endure it, mentally, or you would go crazy. So far, this method of being quiet and trying to relax in his car had served him well.

Johns made it to his office in about twenty-five minutes and it seemed he hit every red light once he got off of the freeway. Surprised it was open, he parked in a spot that he particularly liked and got out of the car. He walked up the steps into his building and opened the door. Walking down the main hall to the elevators brought a few people he knew and so he waved and said hello. Being friendly was also another technique he tried to employ to knock off the stress. He was sure he was about to come up against a bunch of it once he hit the office. He made it to the elevators and pressed the call button. It was slow but it eventually made it there and he stepped in. Johns hit the button for the eighth floor and the doors shut. After a longer ride than what he experienced at the CDC, the elevator came to a stop at the eighth floor and he stepped out when the doors opened. He turned left, and with a short walk, he was at the office. He took a deep breath, trying to etch a steel face for what was about to come, and then he stepped through the door.

Surprisingly the office was quiet. Most agents were at their desks typing away. He walked towards the back of the office, towards where his boss's room was at, and as soon as she saw him she waved him in. He opened the door and she pointed to a seat in front of her desk. She was on the phone and it seemed like she was just finishing up with it. His boss, Jenna Walsh, was about 5' 8" with long blond hair that she kept pulled up. She had soft green eyes that belied the shark behind them. She would tear you a new asshole if that was what was required but she would also be the one who would bake cookies for the office. Her love for the outdoors, especially the water, could be seen with her tanned skin and multitude of pictures showing her skiing, fishing, and just having a good time with her friends. Johns was still taking in her features when she hung up the phone.

"How did it go with the couple you picked up in Indiana?" Walsh asked Johns.

"It went surprisingly well," he responded. "Dr. Boone and I have them down on the fifteenth floor in a holding room. Boone took blood samples from both of them and is currently testing them as we speak. You know how that goes, it could be a while. I told him I would be back in a few hours. What did you find?"

"It wasn't me that found it," she said. "We had our field guys tracking down the vials ever since they were stolen. We were keeping tabs on them before that, of course, and the theft threw a wrench in our plans for acquiring them."

Johns looked at Walsh with a concerned face. She was building up and what was about to come out was going to be good.

"The field team tracked the thieves all the way to the Old Warehouse District in Chicago."

Johns' eyebrows went up in disbelief.

"I know, right?" said Walsh. She continued. "Anyway, the team saw that the thieves were meeting someone in one of the old, decrepit warehouses that litter that area, so they decided to wait and see who else was there. No doubt the thieves were there to sell the vials. The team did not know how many people or groups were in the warehouse so they hung back at a considerable distance. They had just got some surveillance set up in a warehouse nearby when the shit seemed to hit the fan."

Walsh stopped talking and took a drink. A can of Mountain Dew was sitting on her desk right alongside a Snickers. She did love her chocolate. She swallowed and continued.

"The team had the surveillance up quick enough to deduce that there were two groups inside. The first was a group of four black males and they were the thieves. The second group had an undetermined number, and were led by a male of Chinese origin."

Johns started to speak but before he could Walsh held up her hand and answered his question.

"No, no, no. The surveillance team did not recognize him as anyone that we currently have in our database. What they did see surprised them greatly. Like I said they barely had the surveillance up when the shit hit the fan. Suddenly the team saw explosions. It looked like the thieves were trying to get away and one of the cars went up in flames. Another car was driving like a bat-out-of-hell and barely escaped another rocket that was fired. We now believe that rocket was just a diversion to keep the other driver moving quickly. We also now believe that the driver had been infected. You know some of this as you were on the team that was informed of the car in Indiana. By the way, good job with that op."

Johns smiled and nodded. Walsh continued.

"So the team immediately made a choice. They broke into two groups. One followed the driver from the first group. Like I said you know about that because you were called in for the extraction team. The other followed the leader of the second group. Some of the individuals from the second group broke off and so our team only followed the leader. He headed towards the airport and our team followed. They are at the airport right now and they found out what flight he took. It was a personal jet, belonging to a company by the name of *Bio-Tech Beijing*. I have all available agents in the office looking into the company right now. The flight was headed to Paris for refueling and then it had plans for making its way to Beijing as its final destination. I am about to call Paris authorities and see if I can get some cooperation."

Walsh opened her upper left desk drawer and pulled out a book. She opened it and her finger filed down a list until she came to a name and number. She dialed the number and sat back. As it rang she told Johns to go get some coffee and a snack because the call might take a while. Johns nodded and immediately stood up and headed for the door. He grabbed the door and opened it. As he was walking through he heard his boss speak French in a very polite and friendly way to whoever was on the other end of the line.

Johns shut the door and walked out into the main office. Walsh was right, every available agent in the office was busy typing on their keyboards in an attempt to find out what *Bio-Tech Beijing* had to do with this mess. Johns walked to the back of the office and opened a door situated on the back wall. It opened up into a medium-sized break room. The break room had a few Pepsi machines and a few candy machines. It also had a spinning food machine. Johns affectionately called it The Wheel of Death and walked over to it. He spun the machine a few times looking for something to eat. He found a breakfast burrito, not good for his heart but good for his stomach, and put in the $2.50 to buy it. He slid open the door and grabbed it out. He took the burrito to the microwave, popped it in, and hit the fast-timer for two minutes. While the microwave nuked his burrito he walked over to the coffee machine and poured himself a cup. It smelled fresh and tasted quite good. Someone must have just made a pot. The microwave *dinged* and

Johns pulled the burrito out. He sat down in one of the chairs at the break room table and opened his burrito. Although he knew it had more sodium in it then what a normal person should be eating, he dove into it hungrily.

While Johns sat eating his food, he thought about what he knew about the case. Initially, Homeland Security had been tipped about the vials. They had been told that the vials contained a deadly virus. That was it, no other information. They had tracked the vials down and were surveilling the owner when the vials were stolen. That had led into what they were currently dealing with. What did *Bio-Tech Beijing* have anything to do with the stolen vials? Did they create the virus and now try to get it back? Were they the ones footing the bill on the thievery? If so who then created the virus? And for what purpose? That was one thing that they still did not know. The purpose. What could or would the virus do?

Johns realized he was done eating his burrito. He sipped his coffee and then decided that he would take the boss a cup and set it on her desk. She had a Mountain Dew but that wouldn't last long. He poured Walsh a cup and then topped his off. He left the break room and intended to set the coffee on the table and leave. However, when he got there Walsh was already off the phone and she had an excited and nervous look about her. Johns held up the coffee, which he had a cup in both hands, and Walsh got up and opened the door.

"Good news?" Johns asked.

"Well, for now," replied Walsh. Johns handed her a coffee and sipped at his. They both walked back to her desk and sat down.

"The Paris authorities seem to already be looking into our issue," said Walsh. They got a call a little bit ago about a personal jet just sitting at a gate. They immediately feared the worst and so evacuated that area of the airport. After sending in a robot with bomb-sniffing capabilities they determined that there was not a bomb on board. I gave him the tail number we had and it matched. It's the same jet. While I was on the phone with them they said they had a team who was getting ready to board the jet and search it. I told them I would call back later to see if I could get any more details."

"Did you tell them anything about what we are doing?" Johns asked.

"I just told him to watch out for a small silver case. The one the leader was carrying. He said he would let me know what he finds."

8

Detective LaTulip received the call and immediately headed for his car. The airport was about a thirty-minute drive from the precinct but with what was happening at the airport he expected it to take a little longer. Once the U.S. had called him he knew they were into something bigger than just a random spot of violence. Usually, violence was not random. In his experience, there was always something that either led up to the violence or a plan that had been hatched to accomplish the violence. Agent Walsh with the American's Homeland Security Division had called him personally. They had set a personal trust between one another and had counted on each other before. He was hoping this was not going to be any different. He was still in her pocket for a favor and she was calling it in. He had received the call and had immediately filled her in. He wasn't the detective on the case but that would not stop him from showing up, helping out, and subsequently finding out everything that he could. Of course, Walsh would find out as much as he knew. This would make them even again but they would always have the open line of communication established.

LaTulip arrived at the airport about forty minutes later. It didn't take as long as he had thought it would. He parked his car at the passenger drop-off area and left it there. Police officers had a right to do this in the case of an emergency. He walked towards the doors and they slid open noiselessly. He entered and walked towards where the ticket counters were at. He hit the first one and produced his detective's badge. Immediately the woman behind the counter produced a laminated badge with a lanyard and LaTulip affixed it to his person. This badge was used in situations like this because it had a barcode on it that allowed immediate access through the ticketing and frisking area. He showed the badge and bypassed the metal detectors. He made it to the frisking area and swiped the badge. The x-ray machine opened its doors and he passed through effortlessly. He walked down the long hallway and waited for the train to pick him up. The train arrived and the doors opened. He got on board, behind several others, and the door shut. The train sped up to drop passengers off at the various gates. LaTulip needed the last gate and so he stayed on until the end of the line.

Once the train stopped he departed. He took a right and headed upstairs to where the gates were located. Once on the upper-level LaTulip took a left and headed down to gate B-10. As he got closer the crowd got thicker. At one point LaTulip had to start pushing through the crowd just to get anywhere.

"Get out of the way," screamed LaTulip. Some of the passengers moved but not too many of them. Once he finally pushed past the crowd he ran into the police tape blocking off this area. The police had cordoned off this area because of the thought that there was a bomb on the jet. When it was found that there wasn't a bomb on the jet, the police still kept up the tape to help make their job a little easier. LaTulip stopped at the tape and could see a police officer starting to make a small pathway on the other side of the walkway so that passengers could finally start getting through to the other gates.

"Hey!" he yelled at the police officer. The police officer turned around and LaTulip flashed his badge. The police officer waved him in and then turned back around and continued constructing a roped off walkway. LaTulip passed underneath the tape and headed for the gate. Once at the gate another officer was ensuring no one got through. Once again he flashed his badge and the officer let him in. He walked through the gate bridge heading down at a constant angle. Soon he was at the bottom and opened the set of doors blocking him. He walked outside and noticed that the detective in charge was talking to a small team of officers. It looked like they were getting ready to head into the jet. LaTulip had made it just in time. He picked up his pace and headed over towards the lead detective. He got there as soon as the conversation had ended. He signaled the detective before they moved out.

"Hey Detective Remy," he said. Remy looked up and squinted his eyes. "Boss told me to come down and help out," LaTulip said.

Remy's face reddened a little and he spoke up. "What? He doesn't trust me or something?"

"No, it's not that at all," LaTulip said. "He just figured you could use some more help. Do I need to know anything before we go in?"

Remy took a deep breath and sighed heavily.

"We still don't know too much. The robot we sent in did not detect anything that would lead us to believe there was a bomb on the jet. Also, it did not detect anything that would have us believe that there is anything biochemical on board."

LaTulip nodded. Remy snorted, turned, and headed towards the jet.

"Follow me and watch the rear," Remy said with his back towards LaTulip. He didn't need help and he was obviously insulted that his superiors thought this way about him.

Both men walked towards the jet and caught up with the small group of officers that would be going in with them.

"Alright listen up," announced Remy. "Small change of plans. I am going to still be taking the lead but this time Detective LaTulip here will be taking the rear."

Remy pointed to LaTulip and the three officers that were going in with them all turned and looked at him at the same time. LaTulip waved a small pathetic wave, attached a small pathetic smile, and all three of the officers turned back to Remy.

"I want the three of you to stay between us. I will watch the front, LaTulip will watch the rear and I want the three of you to take the sides and anything else we may miss."

Three heads nodded and three guns were pulled from their holsters. The detectives did the same thing and Remy turned and walked towards the jet.

The jet door was still open and the ramp that had been laid through the door for the robot to go in still stabbed its way into the jet. Remy led his team up the ramp and stopped at the entrance to the jet. He took a deep breath, let it out, and then proceeded. He stepped into the jet and immediately looked back into the cabin. It was empty except for a body hunched over one of the seats. He directed two of the officers to go with him and pointed to the last officer and LaTulip to take the cockpit. LaTulip and his officer headed to the front. The door was still half open but you couldn't see into the cockpit very well. LaTulip directed the officer to open the door while he moved in. Gun up, LaTulip scanned the small area. He soon put his gun down. The only thing organic in the cockpit was another dead body. The pilot was slumped over the jet's controls and had dried blood down his face. A bullet hole made its entry right above his right eye and the exit hole out the back of his head had lodged the bullet into another control panel on the side of the cockpit.

LaTulip stepped towards the cockpit door and passed the officer that was with him.

"Cockpit's clear," said LaTulip. "We have one dead."

"Same back here," was the response from Remy.

LaTulip walked to the back of the cabin and joined Remy. LaTulip's officer followed him. Remy was issuing orders for the officers to lock down the jet. The now crime scene was about to be thoroughly investigated.

"Any idea on who the stiff is?" LaTulip asked.

"None right now," Remy said. "I don't recognize him from any of our databases. Hey, Dubois! Bring me the laptop. I am going to run his face through our system." One of the officers in the jet hurried outside to get the laptop.

LaTulip looked at the man hunched over the seat. "It looks like both stiffs went out the same way.'"

Remy looked at the dead man and then nodded in understanding.

"Hey, Mercier! Do we have any Intel yet on the occupant of this jet? What about the pilot?" asked Remy to another officer.

Mercier spoke up. "Not yet, sir. We are still tracking the tail number down. The plane left Chicago, Illinois in the U.S. We are making our phone calls."

Remy nodded. LaTulip touched the phone in his pocket but didn't take it out yet. He thought about calling Walsh but that could wait. He began looking around the cabin. He walked towards the back of the jet, where the bathroom was located, and while he did he reached into his coat pocket. He brought out a pair of gloves and put them on. Once the gloves were on he opened the bathroom door. Completely empty. He started to step out and something caught his eye. He leaned in a little closer to the sink and noticed a long strand of hair sitting in the sink. He popped his head out of the bathroom and eyed the stiff in the seat. He had little to no hair. He looked back at the hair and grabbed it. He put it in a small baggy that he also carried with the set of gloves. He didn't know if he would need more baggies but he only carried one. The officer would hopefully bring back more when he came back with the laptop.

"Got something," said LaTulip to Remy. Remy jerked his head towards LaTulip. He stood up from his position on the floor where he was examining the area. He walked to LaTulip and saw right away what he had found. He also looked back at the dead man and noticed that he had little to no hair.

"This has got to be something," said LaTulip. "Our man here could not have had this fall from his head."

Remy nodded and grabbed the baggy. Being the detective in charge he would handle and log every item that was found. LaTulip was okay with that. He was here for a different reason anyway. LaTulip continued his search. He decided to look in the overhead storage bins. There were only four and so the search was not long. He did not find a small silver case. The officer now came back with the laptop and a camera and Remy was taking pictures of the dead man's face to run through the system. It would be slightly off, with the bullet hole and all, but the system was accurate enough that if he was in there, it would find him. LaTulip stepped past both Remy and the other officers and made his way down the ramp. Once on the ground, LaTulip walked far enough away from the jet that his conversation would not be heard. He wasn't doing anything illegal technically but the relationship he had with Walsh was something he wanted to protect. He called Walsh and the phone rang only once.

"Tell me you have something," she said.

"I couldn't find anything resembling a small silver case," said LaTulip. Walsh let out a small groan.

"However I did find a long hair in the jet's bathroom. Whoever's it is made a big mistake. It definitely is not our stiff's.

Immediately Walsh cut in. "What do you mean "stiff?" He's dead?"

LaTulip continued. "Do you know anything that can help us? Like the passenger manifest? We'll find it soon enough, I suspect, but it would be nice to have a little heads up. Based off of what you told me you had a team already investigating the jet when it took off from Chicago. What did they find?"

Walsh answered immediately. "The passenger should be a one Mr. Li Qiang Hong. He worked for a company called *Bio-Tech Beijing.* We don't have him in our databases. He is either new to the company or we have not associated him with anything heinous yet. We still have our people researching the company now. We have nothing yet."

It was LaTulip's turn to sigh. "Well, we are currently combing the jet. When we have something I will call you. Is there anything else you can tell me?" asked LaTulip.

"We have nothing else other than who he is and that he had something in a small silver case. We believe that something to be very dangerous. We believe it is biochemical in nature."

LaTulip let out a bigger sigh this time and rubbed his forehead. "Okay, well I guess I will keep you informed about what is happening. Let me know if something else comes up on your end."

Walsh agreed and hung up the phone.

Walsh looked at Johns and stared for a moment.

"We need to get a team on the guy who initially had this stuff," she said. "I realize we know a little something about him but my question is why did he have this stuff outside of the lab to begin with? I also get that it was stolen but the vials should have never been at his house. Johns, you are in charge of this team. I want it to be a four-man team. You and two of the other agents that had originally surveilled him are the core. Find one more trusted agent. I want answers in two days. Find out why he had it and who he was going to sell it to. Dismissed."

Donald and Shelly sat on the bed in the room they were still locked in. They stared up at the ceiling and were silent. Donald suddenly got up and walked to the bathroom. He filled both cups with water and returned to the bed. He handed one to Shelly. They both stayed quiet. Then Shelly spoke.

"Donald, we've been in here for two days now. They have run a few tests on us but haven't really said much. I thought they agreed to let us know what was going on."

They both looked at each other and stayed that way for a moment. Then Donald spoke.

"Yeah. You're right. Next time they come in to test us for something we act. Either they tell us what is going on or we get out and don't look back."

Donald reached over the side of the bed and patted the mattress. Beneath it, Donald had set his 9mm. He was still shocked they had never frisked him before they brought them here. Over the past few days, Agent Johns didn't make an appearance. However, Dr.

Boone had found another doctor to help him out. She was tall, blond, and kind of frumpy. She didn't say much but Donald could tell she was intelligent. Some people just have that look in their eyes. After being tested for several days and in several ways, the not being told what was going on is finally what set the Taylors over the line. They were planning on getting out no matter what.

10

Martin Manning did not know that the Department of Homeland Security was watching him. He did not know that they were staked outside his residence right now waiting for him to come home. He definitely did not see the unmarked car parked on the street nor did he notice the two undercover agents walking down the sidewalk out in front of his place. Martin Manning was as high as a kite and he didn't think there was too much that could bring him down. He had been stuck at work for the past two days. Big projects usually brought days like that. The lab had a room where the scientists could set up a cot and sleep. There was a room down the hall where they could take showers and there, of course, was always the 24/7 cafeteria located a floor up. Martin was always prepared and he kept a few sets of clothes in a backpack in his car. His locker at work always had some toiletries just for occasions like this. The job he was working on demanded his time and he gladly gave it.

Martin Manning was as a high as a kite because he knew that all of the sacrifices he had made were about to pay off. The genetically engineered virus that he had been working on in the lab was a success.

It took him a while to create the virus, not only because of the scientific portion of finding the right materials to put together to establish a working virus, but also because he had to do a lot of the work as a secondary job. His main job was at the forefront. He could not get fired and lose access to the only lab in the country that could support his nefarious deeds. He had to keep his main job. If that meant taking a little extra time on creating the perfect weapon, then so be it. Getting the materials was the easy part. They were all right there in the lab. He just had to find the right mix and test it out. Keeping the mixes and what he was doing secret was particularly harder.

Martin was off to a pretty good start so far. Before he was laid up in the lab for two days he was able to get a message out to the buyer that he would be gone for that amount of time. That was it. Just a simple message stating a simple sentence. Often times, after several days locked in the lab completing a large job, security would inspect belongings and pat scientists down. Whoever was paying for the large job didn't want anyone getting away with their secrets. So, before the two-day excursion occurred, Martin was able to sneak out a small, silver case back to his home. Security normally did not pat scientists down and check their belongings as almost any other day was just the normal on the job kind of day. He was able to get the case by with no problems. The four vials he had in the case would be safe at home in his security safe.

Martin pulled up to his home in Manhattan and put the car in park. He would finally be able to get a hold of the buyer and make the transaction. He would be rich soon and there was nothing anyone could do to stop it. He got out of his car, grabbed his backpack full of dirty clothes, and headed for the front door. Martin got to the door and pulled out his key. He unlocked the door and went in. Immediately he knew something was off. The small living room seemed off for some reason. Then he realized what it was. Some of the knick-knacks he had in the living room were not in the right spot. Rather they seemed to have been shifted or moved. Martin knew he had been gone for two days and so this was not his doing. Right away he tensed up. Could the person still be in his home? He walked very quietly and slowly towards the back of the house. Martin was going to check the back door. The front door was fine. It was still locked. The person who had gotten in may have come through the back door. Cautiously he looked around while he was making his way to the back. Seeing nothing else wrong he continued. He had turned the corner leading to the back door and right away he gasped. The back door's jamb had been busted up and the door had been torn from one of its hinges. Again, Martin looked around to see if the person was still in the house. He slowly walked from room to room checking every possible hiding place. Finally, he came to the last room, his study, and it suddenly dawned on him. He swung the door open not caring if someone was in there. He rushed in and his heart sank into his groin. There behind his desk, behind the reproduced Monet painting of *Water Lily Pond*, was his security safe. The door was wide open and all of the contents were gone, including a small silver case.

Martin dropped to his knees and pulled at his hair. He teared up. How could this have all gone wrong? He was set to deal the vials for $5 million. How did this happen? He told no one about what he was doing and no one knew he had taken them to his home. Martin was in the grips of losing his sanity when he heard a noise at the front door. He was still semi-paralyzed when the Homeland Security agents busted through his study door and pinned him on the floor.

"You have the right to remain silent…" said the agent that was cuffing him. Martin was sure that the agent was still talking but he didn't hear him anymore. Martin wondered if the agent had all of his weight on him because he suddenly couldn't breathe. He thought he heard '…do you understand?' right before he passed out.

Agent Johns splashed water onto Martin Manning's face. *How did the guy stay out for so long?* thought Johns. The drive to the Manhattan precinct was luckily a short one but Manning even stayed unconscious when the agents hoisted his body up and took him into an interrogation room. Johns was tired of waiting and so took the water that was on the table in front of him and splashed it on Manning. Manning grumbled slightly. He moved his head a little, rolling it back a forth a few times. Finally, his head lifted and his eyes focused. The first thing he saw was Johns.

"Good morning sleepy head," said Johns. "Rise and shine." Johns left a shitty smile on his face just to annoy Manning.

Martin shook his head a few times and then tried to stretch and stand up.

"Yeah, that's not going to happen," teased Johns. "You are handcuffed to the chair and the table. Do you know why you are in this predicament?"

Martin, a quiet guy, followed his own usual pattern. He shook his head no.

Johns chortled. He knew Manning was lying. But this, as it were, was the game. He had to play it. He had to get Manning to talk.

Martin spoke up. "Can I have some water?" he asked.

"Sure," Johns said. Johns picked up the now empty glass from the table and scraped it against Manning's face. A few drops came off of Manning's face and into the glass. Johns then tipped the glass to Manning's lips. Manning just sat staring at Johns and did not sip from the glass. Johns shrugged and set the glass down.

"Let's make a deal shall we?" Johns asked.

"What? Do I fucking look like Monty Hall?" asked Martin.

Johns went off the handle and flew at Martin. He jumped across the table and that's when the interrogation room door opened. Johns only had a chance to smack Martin across the face before Walsh was yelling at him. Walsh told Johns to leave and Johns put up a good, fake fight about why he should stay. Walsh 'ordered' him to leave and so Johns left. Of course, he slammed the door on his way out capping off the scene. Johns took a few steps down the hall and then entered the viewing room attached to the interrogation room Walsh and Manning were in. He heard Walsh talking to Manning

"Martin Manning. Do you know why you are here?" she asked.

Manning spoke. "Can I have some water?"

"Of course," Walsh said. She made her way over to the glass at the back wall and tapped on it. She sat back down and both of them were silent. Several minutes later there was a knock at the door. Walsh answered it, took the glass of water, and put it down on the table. She slid it over to him and Manning moved his hands in a gesture indicating that he was still on lock-down.

She pulled out a key from her pocket and released one hand. She sat back down. Martin immediately grabbed the glass of water and chugged it. Walsh waited until he was done and then she grabbed the briefcase she brought in with her and laid it out on the table. She opened it, shuffled a few papers around, and then brought out pictures. She set them in front of Manning.

"Who is this man?" she asked.

It was a picture of the man that had died in the car wreck in Indiana. She knew he did not know him but she had to set the stage.

Of course, Martin shrugged his shoulders. He shook his head.

"I have no idea," he said. "Why am I here?"

"You are here because we suspect that you might be involved with a bio-terrorism group that is getting ready to release a virus into the world. Are you helping them?

There it was, all out in the open. Walsh had purposefully done this to catch a reaction. Only, it wasn't her that was the only one looking. Behind the wall of glass was a machine with a video camera. It was watching their every move. In particular, Manning's every move. It could tell, based off of micro-expressions, whether or not a suspect was lying. Johns was currently back with the machine documenting everything that went on. When Walsh let everything out, the computer caught every movement that Manning didn't think was happening. His eyes dilated, his skin got clammy and sweaty, and his body temperature changed.

"He's lying," said Johns.

Walsh got the message through an earbud in her ear. They could communicate this way, if necessary. It was mostly used one way, however, from the viewer to the interrogator.

"Why are you lying to us, Mr. Manning?" asked Walsh.

"I'm not," he replied. He shifted slightly in his chair. The computer caught it.

"Really?" asked Walsh. She once again reached into her briefcase and brought out some new pictures. She moved the other pictures to the side and spread out the new ones. All of them were of Martin Manning.

"As you can see, we have you photographed carrying this silver case around. We believe that this silver case contained the vials that may have held the virus. Our tipoff told us about you and your deal. We know about it so you might as well confess," fibbed Walsh. "And if you don't tell us what we need to stop this, and you get out of here, do you really think that your Chinese contacts are going to let you live?"

Johns knew she was really hitting it now. Once the small lies came out the suspects usually gave in.

"I want a lawyer," demanded Manning.

"Of course," said Walsh. She stood and walked over to Manning's side of the table. She replaced his hand back in the cuff and grabbed the empty glass. She walked over to the door, opened it, and said, "I'll be right back with one. Would you like anymore?" She wiggled the glass and Martin shook his head yes. Walsh smiled and left the room. The door shut behind her and she did a little wiggle in the hallway. She knew she had him.

Walsh opened the door to the viewing room, went in, and then shut the door behind her.

"What do you think?" asked Walsh.

"I think you know what I think," said Johns with a smile on his face.

"Yeah, I think we have him. I just wanted you to say it," said Walsh.

Both smiled at each other.

"Let's give him some time to stew," said Walsh. "The interrogation actually went quicker than I thought. We'll find him a lawyer and I guarantee he'll try to cut us a plea deal. We'll get all of the information we need from Manning. Did you see the way he shifted in his chair when I showed him the pictures of himself?"

"Oh yes," said Johns. "The computer not only noticed that but it also caught the spike in his heart rate. His heart is racing right now."

Martin could not believe what was happening. One minute he was on cloud nine and the next he was in handcuffs on the verge of getting shipped to prison. *Or worse*, he thought. If they considered him a ter-rorist they could probably find some loophole to have him executed. Martin thought about the situation he was in. It was possible the Chinese stole the vials and set him up to take the fall. If that was the case Martin was not going to let the Chinese win that fight. Once his lawyer came he would spill everything that he knew to the authorities. He, of course, would only cooperate if they cut him a deal on prison time. What deal could he get? He didn't know until he talked to his lawyer. His mind ran rampant with the possibilities.

11

Martin was escorted to a holding room where he and his lawyer could have some privacy. Walsh left them in there with two armed agents at the door. She looked at the agents.

"Let me know when they are through. I'll be in my office", she said.

Both guards nodded and responded with a "Yes ma'am."

Walsh walked down to her office and closed the door. She picked up the phone and called Detective LaTulip. It had now been several hours, and although it could take several more hours before the Parisian authorities would know anything, she decided she would try to give it a chance. LaTulip picked up after three rings.

"Hello?" answered LaTulip.

"Detective, it's me, Agent Walsh," Walsh said.

"I figured so. I noticed the overseas number." Walsh was sure she heard a grin in his response.

"Did you find anything else?" Walsh asked.

"We actually found a few things. I was just getting ready to call you. Firstly, I still have not found this small silver case you were talking about." Walsh immediately sighed.

LaTulip continued. "But, as I said before, we did find a long hair in the bathroom of the jet. Once we processed the hair and ran it through our database we actually found nothing. This could be because we don't have the proper profile on this person. So we contacted some friends in Germany to see if they could help. Turns out, they could. The hair belongs to a female by the name of Afsoon Nabavi. She has been involved with the law in some minor altercations involving Germany and their immigration policies. She is not really on anyone's radar for those kinds of things. She just happened to be in Germany's profile database because of who she is linked to, relationship wise. Her boyfriend happens to be Saeed Kazmi."

Walsh interrupted. "You have to be kidding me."

"Not kidding what so ever. He had just recently been spotted in Israel causing all kinds of hell. We believe he was the co-pilot for this particular jet. How they both got on board this jet, well, I don't know. But we believe it was him acting as the co-pilot. We do know that he has had pilot training. He has been known to be involved with flying when it suited the need of whatever organization hired him. Also, we believe that Afsoon was not alone when it came time to kill Mr. Hong and the pilot. The killings show that two individuals were present. Mr. Hong was shot and slumped over his chair. He was shot from the front and fell forward. We believe Afsoon came out of the bathroom, pulled the gun, and shot him. We can place her in the bathroom and the rest fits. As far as the pilot, not only was he slumped over as if he had gotten shot from the side but the forensics show the same story. The blood splatter on the jet wall next to him showed the shot coming from right next to him. It is possible that she somehow got into the cockpit, got right next to him, and then shot him. I, we, believe that

that is not the case. So, we believe that both Afsoon and Saeed were both here. It is possible that they took the case, and, because I cannot find it, makes not only for a good theory but one that could be true.

Walsh spoke up. "So what I am hearing is that known terrorists may be in control over a virus that could have unknown consequences to whomever they want to attack it with? The target more than likely being anyone in the world? Up to, and including, possibly the whole world?"

"Yes," said LaTulip. "We do believe we may have something else that might keep us going in the right direction, though."

"I'm listening," said Walsh.

"We did capture some video surveillance of them leaving this jet and getting on another one at an adjacent gate. The video does not capture their faces but we do get the tail number of the jet. We are currently analyzing the footage and hope to start tracking down the jet soon. I'll let you know what we find."

"Thank you," Walsh said. "I also just want to let you know that we have a suspect in custody that may have been at the start of this whole thing. He is currently with his lawyer in a holding room and I think we may get the information we need. I will also let you know what we find. If this turns out to be really bad, I think we may be informing more of the world about what is going on."

Walsh had just finished eating when one of the agents guarding Manning knocked on her door. She gulped down the rest of her Mountain Dew and stood up. She answered the door and the agent told her that the lawyer said they were ready. She nodded and closed her door. She followed the agent to the holding room and saw that Johns was already there.

"You ready?" Johns asked.

Walsh shook her head yes. "Let's get out of him what we can. We will offer the normal concessions for helping with an investigation but he is not getting out of this totally unscathed. Johns smiled and opened the door. Walsh walked in and took a seat nearest the lawyer. Johns was right behind her and stood at her back. Since they had already played "good cop/bad cop" it probably wouldn't work again. Not only that but they had him where they wanted him so why try that move again? Walsh wanted to show that she was in charge, which she was, but she also wanted to show that the "good cop" shut down the "bad cop". That she had Johns in check. He was just there as a witness to the deal. Both Walsh and Johns were on the same page.

Manning's lawyer spoke immediately. "First off, I want to ensure that Agent Johns, here, is not only reprimanded but some sort of stiffer punishment comes to him. He hit my client and that is not in accordance with the law."

Walsh sat still and spoke gently. "Agent Johns and I have already talked about that incident. He has received punishment and a blemish has been assigned to his record."

It took everything Johns had to keep his smile off his face. He dug his left fingernails into the palm of his right hand just to induce a little pain so he wouldn't smile.

Manning's lawyer nodded and briefly smiled as if he had just won a huge victory. The lawyer continued.

"My client is ready to talk. Before he does I want to see in writing that he was, and is, willing to talk. That he cooperated with this Department of Homeland Security investigation. I want to ensure that the charges will be dropped and he will be set free after completely giving full details on what he knows."

Johns was surprised at Walsh. She was a better actor than he was. If he was in that chair he would have lost his shit. Johns had to control himself as it felt like he would explode at any minute. He focused on Walsh and that helped a little. She sat silent and still in the chair she was in. Slowly she shook her head no and then spoke.

"I can't say you didn't try Mr. Cobb. But you know the law as much as I do. I can write up something stating that Mr. Manning helped with the investigation. I cannot, however, drop all of the charges against him and I cannot obviously set him free."

Manning was practically out of his chair screaming. "That's bullshit!" he said.

Mr. Cobb, his lawyer, grabbed him and pulled him back to his chair. Cobb leaned over to Martin's ear and quietly spoke to him. After a few minutes of hushed tones, scrunched up faces, and one heated word from Mr. Cobb, they discontinued the conversation. Cobb turned back towards Walsh.

"My client agrees to this. He understands that the signed and notarized confession stating that he helped with the investigation will help to greatly reduce his sentence. He is ready to talk after the confession is signed."

Walsh smiled neatly and nodded. "It'll be just a minute," she said. She and Johns both walked out and shut the door.

"How did you keep your cool in there?" asked Johns.

"I knew we had him and I knew the law," said Walsh. "Lawyers always try that bit and it never works. Like I said he knows the law like I do and he probably told Manning he would try and that it probably wouldn't work out. It didn't and so he had to keep his client in check. There is nothing Manning can do now to get out of this. He can only help himself on the back end with less prison time by helping us out to the fullest."

Both of the agents walked down the hall to the notary's office. There they grabbed a basic, canned confession that contained some blanks within it. The basic wording stated that a certain person helped with a certain investigation on a certain day at a certain time. The "certain" blanks would be filled in by Walsh in front of the lawyer. Agent Walsh, Mr. Cobb, and Martin Manning would all sign the document in front of the notary. The notary would then stamp it and it would be official. Then Walsh would get her answers. Along with the basic confession they also grabbed a notary. The notary grabbed her things and followed the agents down the hall.

After the paperwork was completed, Walsh thanked the notary and she left. Johns ensured the door closed and then he came back to the table. He sat down this time next to Walsh and pulled out a digital recorder. He set it on the desk and pressed record.

"Agent Johns is here as a witness and to record this conversation," Walsh said, looking at Manning. Manning did not look like he was happy. Walsh saw this and put the focus back on her.

"I am going to ask you a series of questions Mr. Manning. I need you to answer them honestly and fully. This conversation does not leave this room but we will use what you tell us to aid us in our investigation. Do you understand?"

Manning nodded yes. Walsh continued.

"Have you created a virus outside of your normal work in the lab?"

"Yes."

"Did you bring that virus home with the intention of selling it to nefarious persons?"

"Yes."

"Who were you trying to sell it to?"

"I don't know."

"Mr. Manning?"

"It was to the Chinese but I did not know in particular the person who was going to pick it up."

"You say it was the Chinese but you did not know who the specific buyer was, is that correct?"

"Correct."

"How did you contact the Chinese buyer?"

"Via email."

"Do you still have that email?"

"I remember it."

"I will need that from you."

Manning spoke the email into the recorder. Walsh wasn't sure where they could get with that info, as Mr. Hong was already dead, but any information was good information. Plus, Manning didn't know that his buyer was dead.

"Did you test the virus out on human test subjects?"

"No."

"How did you know it worked?"

"We had some small samples of human tissue in the lab. I used those."

"Mr. Manning, this next question may be more important than any of the other questions. Once again, I need you to be concise, accurate, and truthful." Manning reluctantly nodded

"How does the virus affect the human body?" asked Walsh.

There was an almost imperceptible smile on Manning's face. Johns could imagine him going through scenarios in his mind on how the virus would play out once unleashed onto the world. Manning finally spoke.

"I will keep it in layman's terms. My virus has been designed to attack the melanin in the skin. Every human being produces melanin. The only exception to this is albinism. Those cases differ because sometimes an albino will produce a little amount of melanin and in other cases, there is no melanin. There are several different types of melanin. They can apply to skin color, hair color, or even brain functions. The virus I created can be modified to attack any person with a certain amount of melanin. In other words, my virus can attack anyone in the world."

Both Johns and Walsh had to close their mouths. They realized once he was done that their mouths were hanging open in surprise, disgust, and disbelief.

"I'm sorry?" asked Walsh.

"You heard me right; my virus can kill anyone it wants to based off of the color of your skin."

Even Cobb turned his head and stared at Manning. The room was silent for a few moments and then Walsh got everyone back on track.

"Is there a cure for this virus? Can we stop it somehow?"

"No," was the only response from Manning. Walsh kept going.

"Do you have an affiliation with any terrorist groups?"

"I just made the virus because I wanted the money."

"Mr. Manning that is not what I asked."

"No."

"Are the Chinese the only group you were talking to about this technology? The only ones you were dealing with over the virus?"

"Yes."

"Mr. Manning. Why did you really make the virus?"

Manning smiled and looked at his lawyer. He said, "I think that is all I have to say."

Cobb, scared, shook his head yes. It was a small nod and his hands were slightly shaking. Walsh stared at both of them for a minute and Cobb spoke up.

"I believe my client has told you all that he knows. I think we are done now."

"Okay, sure," said Walsh. "John, go grab the deputy. It is time to put Mr. Manning in prison until the time of his trial. Mr. Manning thank you for cooperating and will we uphold our end of the deal."

Johns had gotten up and let the deputy in. He came over to Manning, unlocked his handcuffs, and stood him up. Once unlocked from the table, the deputy re-locked his handcuffs and walked him outside. Walsh and Johns knew that they would escort him to prison. They also knew that if it got out to those same prisoners and they knew what Manning had done, he might not live long.

Johns ensured the door shut and both he and Walsh looked at Mr. Cobb.

"How can you defend scum like that?" asked Walsh.

"Cobb wiped his brow and then responded. "It's my job, Agent Walsh. You damn well know that." He looked around as if trying to see who was within earshot of their conversation. Only the three of them were in the room and Cobb spoke again.

"But...I'll tell you what. Off the record of course. If what he just said was true then that virus needs to be found and destroyed. Honestly, what he said scared the hell out of me."

Cobb walked toward the door, away from both of them. He turned one last time and looked at both of them. His look was one of sadness and they could tell he was scared. He shook his head and left.

12

Johns let Walsh know that he was heading back to the CDC. He had called Dr. Boone back on the first day of their departing and let him know that he, unfortunately, would not be coming back in a few hours like he had planned. Boone was not fazed in the least. Johns knew that Boone would be engrossed with his work. He figured that if he wouldn't have called that day Boone probably wouldn't have even noticed that he had not come back yet. Now that Johns had something to go on with this virus he was headed back to give Boone some of the news. He could not tell him everything, of course, but anything that related to Boone stopping the virus was fair game.

Johns pulled into the parking lot of the CDC and shut off his car. He got out and once again headed for the side door of the main building. He got in and made his way to the room where they had put the Taylors in a few days before. Boone said that he would meet him down there. Johns swiped his badge and the door unlocked. He entered and saw Boone talking to the Taylors. Boone had the glass wall transparent and he was using the microphone. The conversation seemed a little heated. Boone turned immediately when he saw Johns walk in.

"What's going on?" asked Johns. Boone shut off the microphone and then twisted back towards Johns.

"I am trying to explain to the Taylors why I do not have any more information about them than I did the day after their blood tests. They are very angry with me. They are accusing me of keeping them in the dark. I can barely get a word in with them shouting and yelling at me."

"I might be able to help," said Johns. "Can you make the glass opaque so we can talk?"

Boone eyed Johns and then moved the slider on one of the computer screens. The glass went from see-through to a dark black. He suspiciously eyed Johns. Johns moved in closer and sat in one of the two seats near the computer desk.

Johns spoke. "I am about to tell you something that will not only blow your mind but also scare the shit out of you. We actually found the guy that created the virus."

Boone, still staring at Johns, let his mouth drop slightly. Johns noticed and smiled.

"That's not the good part though. The good part is that he spilled the beans on what the virus is. You ready for this? It's a virus that has been created to attack any individual on the planet. It performs this attack based off of the amount of melanin present in the skin."

Boone spoke up, unbelieving. "Shut up. No fucking way. There has been a rumor of something like that for a while in the medical community, but it was thought of as unicorn-like. In other words an idea that we would never really find. An idea that if found could be dangerous, unstable, and quite frankly something that we don't know if we could control very well. A virus that could attack based off of skin color is something that could literally destroy the whole world."

Johns was shaking his head the entire time in agreement. Suddenly, as if a light bulb went off in Boone's head, he jumped up.

"Now everything is coming together and making more sense!" he said. "The tests I was running on the Taylors weren't coming up with good results. We tested their blood with the sample your team acquired from the wreck in Indiana. However, that subject was a black male and the Taylors are obviously white. There is a large difference in melanin between the two test groups and therefore it would not work on the Taylors." Boone snapped his fingers as if that was the key to allowing a fresh new batch of ideas to flood his head. He smiled and suddenly got very excited.

"It looks like I have some more testing to do," Boone said.

"Well, I am glad you are excited," said Johns. "But I do still have some bad news. According to the creator, there is no cure."

Boone stopped smiling and gave a thousand-yard stare. He snapped back and looked at Johns.

"We will work with what we have. Alongside this new information, we will see if we can come up with a cure."

"Make it quick. We fear the virus is currently in the wrong hands. We have teams on the situation but I do not know when or if an attack will come." Boone nodded and started towards the door. He abruptly stopped.

"I also confirmed that the virus is not currently in a form that facilitates air transmission," he said. "It can be made that way but the form that was in the original subject was injected into his blood directly."

"That is good news for the Taylors then, right?"

Boone nodded and looked back at the darkened glass as if he had forgotten them.

"Do you want to tell them? I know it is good news but they are not happy with me right now."

"Yeah, I'll do it," Johns said. Boone walked back over to the computer and adjusted the glass back to its transparency. Johns noticed that the Taylors were in the middle of backing away from the glass and sitting on the bed when the glass had changed. He went to turn on the mic and Johns told him that he wanted to talk to them in person.

"Okay," said Boone. "I will make sure the gas is ready just in case. Like I said, they are a little worked up."

Johns nodded and walked over to the door. Boone unlocked the door and Johns went in. As soon as he stepped inside the door shut. At about that time Johns noticed that Mr. Taylor was pulling something from underneath the mattress. Johns realized a little too late that it was a gun. He started to pull his and Donald, with a forceful gesture, insisted that he didn't do it. Johns raised his hands over his head.

"I told you," Donald said, "that the only way we were going to cooperate was if you kept us in the loop. You haven't been, so we're leaving."

"Where did you get the gun, Mr. Taylor?"

"Really, that's your first question? You failed to pat us down when you took us a few days ago. We're leaving now."

"Mr. Taylor. Please put the gun down so we can talk. I have some good news but you need to put the gun down."

"Yeah right," said Donald. Suddenly they all heard a hissing sound. Johns slowly went to his knees. From there he made his way to his belly and he stayed motionless.

"What is going on?" asked Donald. From the floor, Johns spoke.

"Please, Mr. Taylor, put the gun down so we can talk."

Suddenly Donald and Shelly felt very dizzy. The gun wavered from Donald's hand and it dropped to the ground. Shelly tried to stand and fell into Donald. He barely grabbed her. He was losing strength fast and slowly got her to the bed so she wouldn't fall to the floor. Donald tried to fight the dizziness and only succeeded in making it worse. The energy he was expending was depleting very fast. He tried to speak.

"What are youuuuuuuu…" was all that he got out. He fell to the floor and was motionless. A little trickle of blood pooled around his head where it had hit the floor. Johns noticed this right before he too lost consciousness.

———————

Boone was watching Johns when he entered the room. He saw the gun being drawn from the bed mattress and immediately his finger was on the button to activate the gas. Boone couldn't hear anything but he knew that Johns was probably trying to talk Donald out of the gun. As the gas entered the room, Johns must have heard it because he slowly started getting closer to the floor. This was his training kicking in. Donald seemed to be wrestling with what to do next when suddenly he must have started being affected by the gas. His wife stood up and almost fell over. She was caught but Boone didn't know how. Donald looked like he was ready to topple himself. Once Shelly was on the bed Donald lost to the gas. He fell over hard and smacked the floor.

Boone let the gas stream shoot out for another thirty seconds and then cut it. He ran over to the speaker on the wall and called for a medical team. He told them to bring three gurneys. They didn't question his request. He ran back to the computer and touched the button that started the exhaust fans in emergency-run. He could hear the fans spin up quickly. There was no need in going in after any of them as the gas would last for a while. They would be zonked out hard. When the gurneys came, he would explain what had happened and they would put them in a recovery room. Once they did that he could get back to working on their little dilemma. Now that he knew more information about the virus he was sure that it would be easier to work with.

13

24 HOURS EARLIER:

Afsoon followed Saeed out of the jet. She was now covered in her burka and kept a respectable distance from Saeed. They had landed at Mehrabad International Airport in Tehran, Iran. They walked about a hundred feet before their boss emerged from the jet. Afsoon knew that this was because they had been sent first to make sure the path was clear. Any attack on them and their boss would just stay in the jet. The jet would then fire back up and quickly depart. That was the way of this business. No one attacked and so the two of them kept walking. They had already received their new orders and were to execute them without delay. Since they had made it to the car without incident, executing the new orders immediately went into effect. Afsoon made it to the passenger door at about the time Saeed was getting into the driver's seat. He started up the car and they took off.

Sanjar Ahmadi walked out of the jet and walked towards the waiting limousine. His two trusted agents had just left for their next assignment. Finding buyers and soldiers for the next assignment would not be difficult. He got into the limo and told the driver where to go.

An hour later he was standing at a non-descript door in front of a run-down large building. This building had not had anyone living in it for a while. As a matter-of-fact, no one had been living in it since his group had kicked them all out. Once they were out he had set up a lab inside. It was located several floors down underneath the ground. This particular lab was used to make biological weapons to supply whoever bid the highest. In the next week, it would be used to genetically alter the virus he had handcuffed to his right wrist. He slowly patted the small silver case and opened the door.

14

Agent Johns slowly opened his eyes. The light stabbed them immediately and he closed them with a grunt. He lifted both his right and left hands to his their respective sides of his head. He rubbed, slowly at first, and then vigorously. His headache was not going away.

"Finally, you're awake, sleepy head," said a voice. Johns had learned from the first time. He slowly opened his eyes. He got them slightly opened and paused. The light filtered in and when he had gotten used to the small amount he opened his eyes wider. Slowly, the room he was in came into focus. He was obviously in some sort of recovery room. There were several beds in the room and a door off the far wall. He presumed that was the bathroom. The window blinds were open and that's where all of the light was coming from. In two of the beds lay two other people. He recognized both of them after a moment. They were the Taylors. Suddenly it was coming back to him. He looked over towards where he thought he heard the sound of the voice that had spoken. There, in the doorway, was Dr. Boone. He was smiling and coming this way.

"I had it," said Johns.

"Yeah I saw that," said Boone. Johns winced at his voice.

"Can you keep it down a little?" asked Johns.

Boone lowered his voice. "Sorry. I know your head hurts now but you will be fine. The gas's side effects will slowly go away. Your head will hurt for a little bit and you might have some muscle cramps. If you experience anything worse than a headache or muscle cramps, let me know. Here drink this."

Boone handed Johns a glass of water. Johns, shaking slightly, stopped rubbing his head and grabbed the glass. He guzzled it.

"Oh yeah. The gas usually makes people thirsty too," said Boone.

Johns nodded. He put his right hand on the back of his neck and started rubbing it.

"How the hell did he get that gun in there?" asked Boone.

Johns shrugged. "I must have made a mistake. I thought I pat them down but with what was going on I must have missed it. That could have gone worse."

"Yeah a lot worse," said Boone.

Johns, knowing he made the mistake, felt dejected. He slumped over slightly. He was tired. Damn that gas.

"How is it going with them?" asked Johns as he pointed at the Taylors.

"They are doing fine as well. They will feel like you when they wake up but other than that, fine. Well, actually, Mr. Taylor will be hurting a little bit more for a little longer. When the gas hit him he fell to the floor hard."

Johns nodded and spoke. "Yeah, I saw that. I also saw blood. Is he okay?"

Boone pointed to Donald's head. "Yeah, he will be fine. Once the medical response team got him up here to this ward they treated his injuries. It was nothing serious. Just a good smack to the noggin."

Boone then pointed in Shelly's direction. "Mrs. Taylor was better off. She fell on the bed. She tried to get up but Mr. Taylor helped her to the bed."

"Yeah I saw that too," said Johns. "So? Have you had a chance to look into the virus now that you know more?

"You three have only been out for a few hours but, yes, in that time I have been able to work with it a little. It is going to take more time. All of us in the lab have devoted our time to it now. Other projects have been pushed off. Agent Walsh called over looking for you. I told her what happened. She was checking in on you but she also wanted to talk to my boss. It looks like she initiated some kind of protocol, due to the time constraints with this virus, and my boss then changed our work schedule and workload. Like I said, everyone is working on this."

Johns smiled slightly. "Did Walsh have a message for me?"

"She said that when you finally wake up that you needed to get back to the office. She has another project for you. Oh yeah, and she also called you a wuss for not being able to take the gas."

Johns chuckled. It hurt his head again.

"I think she was kidding about that last part. No one can withstand the gas," said Boone.

"I know she was kidding," retorted Johns.

Just then a slight movement caught their eye. In the bed adjacent to Johns' bed Shelly was stirring. She turned slightly and tried to open her eyes. She shut them quickly and groaned. She put both hands on her eyes and started rubbing. Boone walked over to her bedside.

"Mrs. Taylor? It's Dr. Boone."

Shelly tried to once again open her eyes. It didn't work and she clamped them shut.

"Take it slowly. Open your eyes when you can. I'll be right here when you do."

Shelly spoke. "What happened?" Her voice was too loud, even for her, and she groaned again. She started rubbing her head just like Johns did.

"You and your husband were in the room with Agent Johns. Your husband pulled a gun on Agent Johns and I had to initiate the gas. That gas knocked all three of you out."

"Where is Donald?" asked Shelly.

"He's right next to you. He's on your right side," said Boone.

Shelly experimentally opened her eyes. She tested the light just as Johns had. Soon her eyes were fully open and she looked over at her husband. Her eyes teared up.

"What happened to him? Why does he have that wrapped around his head?" She was now pointing at Donald's bandage.

Boone answered. "When the gas hit him, it hit him quick. He was still trying to argue with Agent Johns. You husband fell to the floor pretty hard. He hit his head and when we got you guys out of the room we bandaged him up. He will be fine. He shouldn't get more than a headache from it."

"When will he wake up?" asked Shelly.

"He may stay asleep a little longer than you did. Mainly because he did hit his head. As I said, though he will be fine."

Shelly grabbed the doctor's hand. She lightly squeezed and held it for a few moments as if she was trying to stabilize herself. She was still sitting on the bed. He gave a slight squeeze back in reassurance.

Boone spoke up again. "I do have good news for both you and your husband, Mrs. Taylor."

Shelly looked up at him. "What is it?"

"As soon as he wakes up and we get both of you medically cleared, both of you can go home."

"That's great," Shelly said. She paused and then continued. "But what about the virus? Are we infected?"

"Agent Johns, here, was trying to tell you while you were in the holding room," said Boone. He pointed over at Johns and, as if it were the first time she had seen him, she gasped. She didn't realize he was in the bed adjacent to hers.

"Both you and your husband are free and clear from this particular virus."

Shelly now looked up at Boone and smiled slightly. It was good news and even though the outside of her could not get up and dance a jig, the inside of her was doing loops. She would have to do her happy dance later when she felt better.

An hour later Boone's pager went off. He left the lab and headed towards the recovery room. He knew it would be Shelly and he wanted to get them on their way as soon as possible. He stepped through the door and saw that he was right. Donald had woken up. It looked like he was still going through the rigmarole of waking up after being subjected to the gas. Boone knew he would have to explain himself and the situation again and so steeled himself. He explained, once Donald was fully attentive, and asked if there were any questions from either of them. Donald spoke.

"What happens to me now that I pulled a gun on a federal agent?"

Boone answered. "Agent Johns has dropped all charges. You're lucky, actually, that I was there to administer the gas. Without it, the situation may have gone a lot different."

"So do I get my gun back?"

"The answer is yes but you do have to fill out some paperwork. One of the most important pieces of paper you will sign is an NDA. A non-disclosure agreement will basically, legally, ensure that you do not talk about anything that happened here." Boone saw Donald looking at him with a questionable smirk. He saw his mouth start to open and Boone continued before Donald could say a word.

"It's either that or prison time. Actually, it's prison time if you fail to sign all required documents because you did pull a gun on a federal agent. It's also prison time if you fail to keep quiet once the NDA is signed."

Donald's mouth shut right away. Shelly was out of her bed and sitting next to Donald in his. She hugged him and rubbed his back. She must have said something when she hugged him because he nodded slightly and hugged her back. Boone saw this as a fitting time to speak.

"Are both of you ready to leave?" The Taylors shook their head collectively.

"Good. I will get someone from the medical staff in here to check you out. Once that is completed you can sign your release forms and NDA and you are free to go home."

"How do we get home?" asked Shelly. "You guys brought us here in your van."

"The CDC will provide air tickets for you to make it home. They will also set up transportation for you from the airport back to your home. I hope that works for you because it is the best we can do. I am truly sorry that the situation went down the way it did. I am glad for your good news on being healthy."

Both of the Taylors nodded and Boone left. He stopped at the nurse's office and talked to one of them about discharging the Taylors. He was happy to get back down to his lab.

PART TWO

15

Johns made it back to the office and found Walsh waiting for him. She was in her office and drinking a Mountain Dew. She waved him in and he opened the door and took a seat at her desk.

"I have some news for you," she said.

Johns eyed her suspiciously and said, "Okay…"

"Don't worry I think it's a good thing, Agent Johns. I just got off the phone with the director and he just approved an op. I want you to lead the team."

Johns knew she was building it up and that she was going to finish, but once again he eyed her suspiciously and said, "Okay…"

Walsh chortled and sighed. She said, "We have a good lead as to where the silver case may be. Intel has delivered some information to us, information that you will be choking on soon in all of its glorious detail. For now, however, settle for this: the man you are going to be looking for is named Sanjar Ahmadi."

Johns' jaw dropped. "You mean the leader of the terrorist group known as *The Black Scythe*? How did he get his hands on it?"

"It seems the faces of the couple that we were trying to track down, Saeed and Afsoon, were seen not long ago within one hundred feet of Mr. Ahmadi. A camera at the Mehrabad International Airport in Tehran, Iran caught them leaving a personal jet. Shortly thereafter Mr. Ahmadi left the jet with a shiny silver box clutched in his grubby little paws. He got into a limo and drove away. From there we tried to work with our contacts on tracking them down and got little from them. For one the cameras are few and far between. More times than not they simply don't exist. Also, they are not very comfortable tracking down men like that in their country. They didn't want to help too much."

Johns interrupted Walsh. "Let me guess, we just so happen to have people over there who would help?"

Walsh smiled and nodded slightly. Johns said, "I don't think I want to know."

"Probably not," said Walsh. "However you may find out more than you want to anyway during this briefing. I need you in the briefing room at 0700 tomorrow. Tehran is eight and a half hours ahead of us. After the brief, the not so short flight will get you to the forward operating base, and from there you will meet up with your team. You will have a little time to set up with them but for the most part, the plan is set. Of course, as the leader, you can adjust on the fly as necessary. I don't think I have to remind you, but just in case: the briefing is in the conference room in the basement."

Johns nodded and stood. Walsh stood also and they shook hands. She had a firm grip. Almost stronger than Johns'. He smiled and told her he would see her tomorrow. She smiled back and said nothing.

Johns left the office and headed for home. Being a part of this from the beginning had put him in a position to allow Walsh to consider him for this new job. He was a part of security when he was in the Army. He had gotten out of the military, and because of that training, he had landed this job. He did not think that he would be operating exactly like that again. His team was no doubt going to be made up of ex-military or even active duty military members. Taking orders is what they did and so he did not expect any problems. He was suddenly excited about meeting his new team.

16

The Taylors had finished off their paperwork and had been discharged. The CDC had then gotten them a ride to the Hartsfield-Jackson Atlanta International Airport. They didn't have much to do when they got there. Because they did not have anything on them when they were taken, the CDC provided a fresh set of clothes, some fresh ID's, and a little bit of money. The ID's did not establish a new identity for them, they were just their old identities in a newer package. The flight was on Delta and it was non-stop. The Taylors arrived back in Indiana after about a one and a half hour flight. They then were once again provided transportation back to their house.

The first thing that the Taylors noticed when the taxi dropped them off in front was that the tree in their front yard had been burned. Nothing was in the front yard anymore but you could tell that something had happened. The yard was burned and you could see the skid marks on the front lawn. Donald turned to Shelly.

"The CDC does not want us to talk about what happened and yet our front yard looks like a bonfire raged out of control."

Shelly nodded. "We'll have to wait until spring but we can get it fixed up Donald. We'll plant more grass and the burn marks on the tree and grass will grow out. It'll be fine."

Donald pursed his lips slightly like he was thinking of something to say and then he just nodded. They both walked into the house and crawled up the stairs. They made it to the bedroom and they fell onto their bed together. They were both exhausted and the feeling of being home and in your own bed was almost something quite heavenly. Donald turned over to his wife and just looked at her. She was beautiful. Even when she was exhausted she was beautiful. He decided he might actually have a little energy left in him. He rolled a little closer to her and cupped a breast. Shelly, startled at first, rolled away. Then, suddenly realizing she had more energy too, rolled closer to him. He touched her face gently and kissed her on the mouth. She pressed back and the kiss was long and passionate.

"I guess I didn't much feel like this when we were locked up," said Donald.

Shelly nodded and stuck her finger to his lips. She kissed him this time and the kiss was even longer. The next thing they knew they had stripped and were messing around like teenagers. After they were finished they fell into a deep, comfortable sleep right next to each other.

17

Johns came out of the briefing in the basement with his head full of so much Intel that he thought it was going to burst. He had been briefed on Sanjar Ahmadi and what he looked like now. He had been given the location of the lab where Ahmadi was expected to be. He even got a briefing on his new team. All four of them would be at the forward operating base waiting for him. They would be receiving this same brief before he got there. He made it to the bathroom in time and unzipped his fly. He had to piss badly and the brief had taken forever. Now, it seemed, only his head was primed to burst. He finished, washed his hands, and left the bathroom.

He met Walsh in the hallway on the way back towards the briefing room. Since the brief was over everyone was filing out. She stopped him to talk. She saw the look in his eye and knew the information he had received was a lot to take in. She grabbed him by the arm in reassurance.

"Don't worry, you'll do fine," she said.

"I know," said Johns. "It's just a lot to take in and I want to obviously do well. Literally, the whole world is counting on us, even if they don't know that they are."

Walsh smiled. Johns said, "I am going to head home now and pack a few things. If you need me, call. Otherwise, I will be at the airport in three hours." Walsh hugged Johns one last time and watched him walk off towards the elevator.

Johns made it to the airport in time and had no issues getting through security and frisking. He got to his gate with ten minutes to spare and decided to get a quick sandwich. He found a deli place just two gates over and he stopped there. They made his sandwich quickly and Johns paid for it and a bottle of water. He walked back towards his gate and the intercom was just finishing up with announcing the boarding procedures. His seat was in section 'C' and so he would be one of the last to board. Johns found this humorous that the passengers in the back were the last to board. It made no sense to have the boarding set up this way. What it did create was chaos and angst when the back passengers had to crawl over and around the front passengers to get to their seats at the back of the plane. Johns thought he had seen why it was set up this way on a TV show called *Mythbusters*. They attempted to explain why it actually worked but Johns couldn't remember the reasoning.

The intercom called for his section to start seating and he moved with the rest of the passengers. *This is going to be a long flight,* thought Johns. He handed the man at the ticket counter his ticket. He swiped it and let Johns through. Down the boarding ramp and into his assigned seat was just the start of a rather boring flight for Agent Johns.

The plane landed at Mehrabad International Airport. Johns departed and headed to baggage claim. He had only claimed one small suitcase. Soon, he saw it on the conveyor and he grabbed it. He turned to head outside and saw a man holding a sign with his name on it. He walked up to the man.

"Yes, I'm Johns," he said.

The man smiled and shook his hand. "Mr. Johns, I will be your driver. If you would follow me please."

Johns followed him outside. The driver walked to the back door of a sedan and opened it.

"If you please," said the driver.

Johns nodded and got in. The driver shut the door and went around to the driver's side and got in. He started the car and with a jerk, took off. The car ride was not unpleasant. Nor was it stimulating. The driver did not talk. He just drove. This gave Johns and opportunity to check his email from his phone. It was empty, which was odd. Walsh must have taken care of the minor details for him, knowing he would be out. The car ride lasted about an hour. The car turned down an unnamed road and suddenly stopped. In front of them was a gate blocking their path. Two armed guards approached the vehicle. The driver spoke in English and Johns thought he heard his name. One guard stayed with the driver while the other one walked to the back door on the passenger side. He opened the door and spoke to Johns.

"Hello, sir. Last name?"

"Hello. Johns."

The guard nodded and motioned for Johns to exit.

"Sir, if you would please step out of the car."

Johns followed and was soon standing next to both guards. The driver smiled, waved, and then drove off. One guard walked off while the other guard looked at Johns.

"Sir, if you would please wait here with us. My compadre is going to touch base with your contact and we will have you at the site in no time." The guard walking away from Johns entered a small shack at the side of the path. Soon after, he came back to the small group.

"Colonel Harris is on his way."

"Thank you," said Johns.

Colonel Harris showed up ten minutes later. He pulled up in a jeep. He put the jeep in park and jumped out. The guards acknowledged him with a salute. He saluted back and approached Johns.

"Welcome Agent Johns," he said.

"Thank you, sir. I am glad to be here. Sorry it took so long. The flight was quite long."

"That's okay. I understand. Jump in the jeep and we can talk on the way back to the compound."

Harris motioned him on and Johns followed. He jumped into the passenger seat and Colonel Harris started the jeep up. He turned around and headed back towards the compound.

"So I understand you have already been briefed back at Homeland Security?"

"Yes, sir."

"Good. Your team has also been briefed and are anxiously chomping at the bit. When we get back to the compound I'll show you to your room. I want you to shower and get some sleep. We are going to execute the mission tomorrow night at 2200 so that leaves a little bit of time during the day for you to talk to your team and plan a strategy. All four of their files are on your bunk. They all have strengths and weaknesses. You won't get to know them that well in such a short amount of time but their files should help you derive a coordinated team approach. Any questions?"

"No, sir."

"Good," said the Colonel with a smile on his face.

The jeep pulled up to the compound and Harris shut it down. They both jumped out and Johns followed him through the door. Once in, they took an immediate right and Harris stopped at the third door on the left. What little Johns saw of the interior of this building made him think of a dorm hall. Every room would be filled with soldiers. Maybe some of the rooms were a little more spacious or fancy for those with higher rank but Johns was sure he was getting the same treatment as any other soldier.

"This is your room," said Harris. "This is your key." He handed Johns a key. It was silver and plain. Nothing special about it. It had his room number on it and that was it. He was surprised it was not a key card.

"Your team is booked in the rooms around you." Harris pointed to four other rooms adjacent or next to Johns' room. "Like I said, you'll meet them tomorrow. I will call you tomorrow at 2000. I'll expect you to be ready with your team by then."

Colonel Harris started to walk away and then stopped. "Oh yeah, the cafeteria is just down the hall. When you get to the end of this hall take a right and then a left. You'll see it. Or just follow your nose." Harris turned back and walked away.

Johns stood for a minute watching him walk away. He was stout and he walked like he had a purpose. He stood straight and his hands stayed clenched the whole time that Johns watched him. Johns knew this was a tough man that wouldn't take any shit.

18

Sanjar Ahmadi listened carefully as his spy reported what he had found out. Instead of scrunching up his face in disbelief and anger, Ahmadi smiled. If the Americans were coming for him then he would be ready. He would not be able to get all of them but he would take out most of them. Most of them were of the same cloth and that cloth could now be cut. The small silver case that he acquired had four vials in it. He had his team working with all of them but the initial focus had been with the one that would help to wipe out the white devils. His team had worked quickly and found out that the virus was not lethal via air. Ahmadi had soon changed that. His team had not only got it to work with air dispersion but they also rigged a way to get it to the mass public. The Americans coming after him would soon find out that they were about to spread the most deadly virus that was ever known to man.

Ahmadi dismissed his spy. He ran off and Ahmadi called for his second in command.

"Are the dispersion units set up?" Ahmadi asked.

"Yes sir," answered his second. "They are set up at every main junction in this place. Every time a hallway meets another and at every main door. They are set to go off with the detection of movement. Of course, this key fob will initiate those sensors once we are long gone."

Ahmadi's second handed him the key fob. Ahmadi's eyes increased in size as he stared at the device. It was as if he had just found a large clump of gold.

Ahmadi tore away from the key fob and slipped it into a pocket. He then spoke to his second. "Start packing everything up and get it to the other lab and continue production. I want the rest of the viruses ready to go in three days. That includes the air dispersion capability."

"Yes sir,' said his second and then he ran off quickly.

Ahmadi grinned and thought to himself, *This should let the Americans know not to fuck with me.*

19

Johns woke up to the light piercing through the window. He tried to shut his eyes but they were already shut. He pressed them even tighter together but that didn't help. He decided it was time to get the day going. He was going to meet his team today and he was excited about it. First thing's first though. He rose from his bed and grabbed some underwear from the measly pack he brought. He started the shower and let it run for a minute. After it had warmed up and he was stripped of his clothing, he jumped in. He washed up quickly. The entire time he thought about what he was going to say to his team and how they would respond to him. He thought that they would all have a different reaction. Hell, they all had different personalities.

Johns soon was out of the shower and getting dressed. He started smelling breakfast from down the hall. He thought he smelled bacon and his stomach rumbled. Johns was definitely hungry after the flight yesterday. He strapped on a pair of boots and headed for the door. Johns walked out of the room and almost ran into someone. He looked up and saw one of his teammates. He recognized her from the pictures in her file.

"Hello," Johns said.

"Hello sir," came the reply.

"You heading to breakfast?" Johns asked.

"Yes, sir."

"Can I join you?"

"Of course, sir."

Johns remembered from her file that Amanda Collins was active duty Air Force. She was a 1st Lt and would be his second in command. Although she was a leader, she also had skills that would be invaluable to this team, as would all of the team members. She knew Farsi as well as having been trained in electronics. Her electronics training got her the nickname 'Wire Biter.' It was usually shortened to just Wire. John thought it was perfect that he ran into her first.

"So, Lt Collins, will the rest of the team be joining us?" asked Johns. He assumed she recognized him as well.

Collins had obviously recognized her boss and responded as such. "Yes, sir. I let them sleep in a little more. They are meeting us in the cafeteria in thirty."

"Sounds good. Gives us a chance to get on the same page," said Johns.

***

Johns and Collins immediately fell on the same page. Johns had confirmed that the entire team had received the same brief. They were all aware of where they were going, what they were doing, who they were trying to get and all of the dangers associated with the mission. Almost thirty minutes had passed when Johns noticed the other three members of his team come into the cafeteria. They acknowledged Collins and got in the chow line. Soon they had their food and they came over to the same table where Collins and Johns were sitting. All three of them sat down at the same time. Two of them went into a prayer right away. The other sat watching until they were done and then he started eating.

"I'm glad we could all make it," said Johns. "Please keep eating and chime in when you see fit."

The member that hadn't prayed was ex-Army. When he was in he was a Sergeant First Class. He had gotten out and was paid to take jobs like this one. He helped out the military but was no longer affiliated with them. Other agencies paid him to perform other tasks. His specialty was explosives. Johns didn't know if he would need an explosives expert but having one was not a bad thing. His real name was Thomas Blake but his nickname was 8-Finger, although it was mostly shortened to just 8. He had all of his fingers intact so it was sort of a joke.

The other two team members finished praying and commenced eating. They ate voraciously as they were not small individuals. These two, Edward and Owen Hunter, were twins. They had joined the Marines together. The Marines had a program where you could sign up with a buddy and wherever you went your buddy went too. Your buddy, of course, had to qualify for the same thing as you but the program allowed for you and your buddy to get the same job. These two brothers had signed up together, had been stationed together, and had only competed with each other. They were two of the best Marines no matter where they went. Naturally, they got sent to Marine Recon School. There they excelled in everything. Their specialties were hand to hand combat, although they were trained with several different kinds of weapons. The only difference Johns found in their files was that one preferred a sniper gun and the other liked close range shotguns. Their nicknames, Ghost and Scatter, came from that one difference.

Johns smiled as the three of them continued eating. He could tell that although they were eating they were intently listening.

"Ok here we go," said Johns. "I know all of you were briefed the same thing so no need to get into that again. I want this conversation to concentrate on the actual mission of getting into the building where the targets are located. We'll leave here tonight at 2200. We will be dropped off at the rendezvous point 2 klicks outside of the target building. After the hike in, I want you, Ghost to take the building opposite our target. Our Intel says it's empty but be careful. I want eyes up high watching our backs. From there I will lead Wire, 8, and Scatter into the target building. I want Scatter to take point. I want access to the building to be quiet but I want your shotgun at the ready to breach if necessary. I will follow Scatter and then I want 8 to follow me and then Wire to take up the rear. We will sweep each level until cleared or until we find the target."

"We will enter and exit as one team. If we need to split up for any reason I will make that call based off of the situation. Remember to keep your mics on and if we do get split up we meet back at the rendezvous point. Everyone copy?"

All heads shook affirmative. The twins were almost done eating and 8 wasn't that far behind.

Johns spoke again. "Because we are not leaving until 2200 tonight we have some time to relax. Decompress however you see fit but I want everyone ready by 1930. Colonel Harris will call by 2000 and then we will head over to the armory to gear up. Once we receive the Colonel's call I want you, Wire, to contact the garage and get them to pick us up at the armory. From there they drive us to the rendezvous spot and, well, you guys know the rest."

"Copy that sir," said Wire.

"Yes sir," said 8.

The twins answered in unison, "Aye aye, sir."

"Dismissed," said Johns.

Everyone stood quickly and picked up their trays. After dropping them off to get washed they headed out to do whatever they wanted for the rest of the day. Johns was elated to see that he had such a great team to work with. It was true that he hadn't worked with any of them before but he could tell that they would do their jobs and do them efficiently. Johns decided that for the next few hours before lunch he was going to check this place out. He stood, took his tray over to the washing area, and dropped it off. He headed out of the cafeteria looking for something interesting.

20

It was about 1800 when Johns stirred from sleep. After breakfast, he had found a break room where some of the soldiers had been hanging out. He saw that the break room had a few pinball machines in it but it also had two billiards tables. Several soldiers were milling about the table and Johns asked if he could join. Soon the soldiers were getting schooled but having a good time. Not long after Johns had started playing Collins drifted in. She challenged him to a game and he agreed. Johns didn't know how Collins played so he let her take the lead. He soon learned that that was a bad idea. She was good. He was good too but letting her lead left him in the rear. After the first game, things got interesting. Soon money was on the table and suddenly the crowd seemed bigger to Johns. He thought he caught Colonel Harris' face in the background but then it disappeared. The table next to the one they were using was abandoned in favor of watching what was going on at this table.

They were three games into it, after the first free game, and Johns was tired of losing money. Soon Collins noticed and to help him save face said that she had something else that needed doing. They shook hands and the crowd dispersed. It was almost lunchtime then and he headed towards the cafeteria. There he saw the members of his team eating together. He came over to the table and asked to sit. They motioned him towards a seat and he sat. They talked but not about work. The talk was about their family they missed back home or something they saw on the internet. Work talk was not part of the relaxing that they were trying to do. Relaxing was a very important part of pre-gaming a mission. You had to get your body right as well as your mind. Johns knew that when 1930 came around they would be all business.

He left them after about a two-hour lunch and headed back to his room. He figured he would read for a while and then take a nap. He knew that they might be out all night and every ounce of strength may be needed depending on what they encounter. Although Intel could get you a lot, there were just some things that it couldn't see. Inside the target building for one thing. Intel did not have anyone on the inside. All of the Intel that had been acquired was external to the target building.

Now that Johns was up he thought he smelled dinner. *Man, these walls are thin,* he thought. He got up, got dressed, and headed for the cafeteria. This would be the last meal before they headed out. He once again saw his team while he was there. This time, though, Wire and 8 were having a light meal. Ghost and Scatter had a plate full. They were gorging once again.

Wire looked up at Johns staring at the twins. "They worked out this afternoon," was all she said.

Johns nodded, smiled, and sat down.

Johns started to eat and Wire spoke up. 'Sir, we were talking about something before you showed up and we wanted to run it by you."

"Okay," said Johns.

"Well, we noticed that during our conversation from breakfast you didn't mention what your nickname would be. We will have constant radio comms the entire time and you need to have a nickname."

The rest of the team chuckled slightly and Johns looked around. He was waiting for this. He wanted his team to give him a nickname. That's how it worked. Considering they had never worked together before, the team had not had a chance to name him. By the chuckles at the table, he knew they had come up with something that was not so flattering.

"Okay, I'm all ears," said Johns.

"Well sir, after today's fiasco with playing pool…"

Oh no, thought Johns. *Here it comes.*

"We figured you could be Shark."

The rest of the team erupted into laughter. The entire cafeteria looked their way and then turned back around.

"Why, because I'm so good?" asked Johns.

Once again his team lost it. They were laughing so hard their faces were red.

"Oh, of course, that's why, sir," said Wire with a shit-eating grin on her face.

Johns held his composure for a few seconds and then grinned.

"Hey," he said. "She's good." He pointed towards Wire.

The team wouldn't stop laughing. Knowing that this meant something to the crew, he obliged.

"I love it. Thanks," he said sarcastically.

Still laughing the team picked up their trays and once again deposited them to be washed. Johns looked at his watch and saw that it was already 1900. Soon he would be calling his crew into his room and waiting for the Colonel to call.

At 1930 sharp, Shark had swung his door open. There, standing in the hallway, was the entire team. They were standing at parade rest near the far wall. "Fall in," said Shark and stepped aside as the team bustled into his room.

At 2000 on the dot, the phone rang. Shark answered it and had a conversation with the Colonel. It lasted for only five minutes and then he and his crew were filing out of his room. Once they made it to the lobby of their building, Wire stopped to pick up a phone. The rest of the team continued walking. They left the dorm building and headed for the armory. Wire finished her phone call to the garage and quickly followed her team.

The walk to the armory was not long, ten minutes away, and by the time they got there the jeep from the garage was already in place. The armory let them in and showed them into a caged area. From there the soldier manning the armory handed everything to them that was on his invoice request from the Colonel. As each and every item was handed to them, they put it on. Each team member received a web belt. They all donned their belts and awaited the next item. A military issued 9mm was next, as was standard. This gun was secondary to the primary gun they would receive. For this gun, each member also received three clips, which held 17 rounds each. These got put into their web belts. Next came the earpieces. Each earpiece in the group was connected to all the other earpieces in the group via a specified frequency. Shark had the team take five minutes to perform comm checks. Ghost's earpiece had a crackle in it and so they swapped it out. Everyone performed comm checks with him again and this time it worked perfectly. Shark would have them perform comm checks one last time once they were at the rendezvous point. The only difference with his earpiece, as compared to the others, was that he could swap it to another frequency and talk back to the FOB. Next came the flak jacket. This jacket was meant to stop small ammunitions fire and some medium sized ammunition fire. It was not guaranteed that a larger round would not penetrate. The entire team picked out their size and donned the jacket.

With two items left, Shark looked at his team. He could tell they were ready for this mission. Not one of them looked scared. He knew their heads were in the game and that they would perform at their best. Their lives were on the line, as well as his, and he silently promised himself that he would get them all out of there alive.

The armory soldier started walking around handing out the team's primary weapon. This weapon was based on what their primary job was going to be. Ghost was first and received a sniper rifle and a bandolier. The Barrett M98B fired .338 Lapua Magnum rounds and weighed only 12.4 pounds. It was a bolt action, single shot and did not pack as much of a punch as a .50-caliber sniper rifle but the location where Ghost would be at did not require much. Plus the lightweight was ideal for not only the hike into the target location but also so Ghost could move a little easier on the roof of the building if necessary. The rifle also contained a scope with a flip down filter for night shots. Ghost was given 25 rounds and he was able to find a place for them in his sniper oriented bandolier.

His brother, Scatter, was given his shotgun and a bandolier. This shotgun, the AA-12, shot 12-gauge shells and it was an automatic. The shells were contained within a 32-shell drum magazine. Scatter was given two drums. One of them he attached to his gun right away and the other was able to attach to his web belt. He was then handed ten rounds of exotic shells. These shells were to be used in special cases. Within this group of ten, there were two door-breaching shells. These shells were specifically made to remove hinges and locks from doors. The group of exotic shells also contained five armor-piercing incendiary rounds. These shells were meant to pierce through armor and they have a tip that will explode and burn at 3000 degrees. The last four shells comprised of two flechette shells and two rubber ball shells. The flechette shells contained 28 small dart-shaped projectiles used to normally to get through brush. Scatter didn't think he would need these. The rubber ball shells contained 3 rubber balls that were less than lethal and were used to stop, not kill, the enemy. Scatter put these ten shells into his bandolier.

The rest of the team, Wire, Shark, and 8 received Colt M4A1 carbines. These assault rifles had a forward grip handle and a red dot sight. They used 5.56 NATO rounds and all three members were handed three magazines which carried thirty rounds each. Each and every member of the team checked their firearms. Primary and secondary guns were checked and then loaded. Once this was completed they were stowed for the hike. The last item given to each member was a helmet. Each member picked a helmet based off of size. They put them on and then strapped them under the chin. After all of the equipment was handed out Shark called them all out to the truck. It was running just outside the door. The driver of the truck was in his seat and ready to go. Shark jumped into the back and his team followed. Soon they were traveling down a path that led to the front gate. The driver of the truck radioed the front gate and the guard there let them pass. Once they passed the gate, they had about a thirty-minute drive across bumpy terrain to get to the rendezvous point.

21

The truck arrived at the rendezvous point. Shark's team jumped out and immediately the truck vanished. Each team member crowded around Shark. They took a defensive stance and every team member kept an eye on their surroundings. The area was clear, as expected, but you still had to be on your guard. Shark and his team performed their comm checks. There were no issues this time and Shark swapped his earpiece and contacted the FOB. They answered that they could hear him loud and clear. Shark then watched as everyone on the team readied their primary weapon. They all performed their final checks on the weapons. They did not expect any interference on the way there but, again, you always had to be on your guard. With comm checks successful and each weapon primed, Shark led his team out. They started the two-klick walk at a good speed. At this rate, they would hit the target building in roughly 25 minutes. Of course, it may take a little longer as they would at some point have to weave in and out of buildings.

The rendezvous point was out in the middle of the desert. It was about a klick and a half from the start of the small town where they were headed but it was very dark out here and they were satisfied that no one could see them. Still, the line-up that Shark had established held tight. Ghost led the group. Shark followed behind him and then it was 8, Scatter, and Wire took up the rear. They kept up their pace until the small town came into sight. Shark stopped the group and everyone took a knee. Although they were listening intently every member kept one eye looking around them.

"Almost there team," said Shark. "Remember the plan. Once we get close to the target I will signal for Ghost to take his place. We will provide cover fire if necessary. However, I want to get him to the building quietly if possible. The others will follow me. We are almost to the cover of buildings now. They may give us cover but they could also provide civilians. This will be a problem. Follow me and watch for my hand signals."

Everyone on the team quietly acknowledged Shark and he started them off again in the direction of the town. Soon they stopped at the first building. Everyone pushed against the side and Shark stuck his head out. It was clear and he motioned for them to follow. There was no lighting on the streets, except for the moon, and so Shark and his team did not encounter anyone. They moved, however, as if they could at any minute. After approximately 6 minutes of quietly skirting buildings, Shark stopped the team. The target was just around the corner of the building they were hiding behind. Shark stuck his head out and saw no one. He did, however, hear noises coming from the building. He motioned for the rest of the team to take a position to give cover fire if necessary. He then motioned for Ghost to take his place.

Ghost ran off to the building adjacent to the target building. The team intently watched the building and the rooftops. No one was in sight. Ghost skirted objects and tried to hug the buildings. He made it to the building and climbed the outside to make it to the roof. The ladder outside was the only entry to the roof and so he began setting up immediately. When he was ready he called Shark.

"Shark, Ghost. In place and ready." Ghost said silently into thin air. His earpiece picked it up and transmitted it to Shark and the team.

"Copy," said Shark. "We're moving out."

Shark waved for his team to move forward. They followed him and soon they were at the front door of the seemingly empty building. Shark could still hear noises and indicated so to his team. They acknowledged that they too could hear noises. Shark tried the front door and it was locked. Well, he had to try. It looked like this was going to be a louder entry that he had wanted. He gestured for Scatter to come up. Scatter was about to load the breaching shells into his shotgun when 8 waved them off.

"Shark, 8. It looks like we could bust this window out and crawl through. It would be a hell of a lot quieter than busting down the front door."

"8, Shark. I copy. Team, the front window is now the point of entry. Ghost, follow our asses."

"Copy Shark."

Shark and his team shifted from the front door to the front window. It wasn't a large window and Shark was surprised the glass was still intact. A small hit from his rifle butt and 8 was able to break the glass. Quietly and carefully the team removed shards of glass from the window. When it was clean enough for them to pass through, Shark stuck his head in. There was some light coming through and Shark looked around. He saw nothing that looked like an immediate threat and so he carefully started to climb through the window.

"Maintain original line-up," said Shark as he crawled through. Next was Scatter, then 8, and then Wire came last covering the rear as per the original line-up. After all ground team members were through, they looked around the room they were in. It looked to Shark as if it were a type of lobby. It hadn't been used as a lobby for some time now. Shark could see cases of something stacked all around and it was obvious that the room had been recently used. The light that was dimly shining into the lobby was coming from the back of the room. Shark used two fingers to point to his eyes and then to the back of the room. He was telling his team to maintain awareness and keep their eyes open for anything. They advanced on the light and came to a 'T'. Shark could now see the light was coming from both sides of a hallway. He stopped his team and had Wire advance. When she came up she held to one side of the wall while Shark was on the other side. She instinctively knew what he wanted. Shark spoke deadly quiet even though he was on the other side of the small room. Their earpieces would still pick up their voices.

"Wire. Looks like this is what I had dreaded. I don't like splitting up but it might be better for us. I need you to take 8 and take the right hallway. I will take Scatter and head down the left. This way we can watch each other's asses. Keep me up to date on your status."

"Copy," whispered Wire.

Both Scatter and 8 fell in behind their respective leader. Shark and Wire turned into their hallway and their teammates subsequently followed.

As soon as the team had stepped through the window, a motion sensor activated. Soon a practically invisible, non-odorous mist slowly seeped into the hallway. The air dispersion unit was set up at the 'T' at the back of the lobby as this was the most obvious place for someone to enter. Other dispersion units went off throughout the building as well, but they were no longer needed. The team had already been coated with the virus. It would not live long on the outside of their clothing or on any of their gear. It would, however, reproduce inside their bodies and then be easily spread through the simple act of breathing. Coughing or sneezing would be an even better method of transmission. It wouldn't take but a few days and the virus, altered to act upon and look for a certain range of melanin in the skin, would destroy its target.

22

As soon as Shark and Scatter lost eyesight of Wire and 8, Shark immediately contacted them via radio.

"Wire, Shark. You copy?"

"Copy," came the reply.

"Roger. Now out of eyesight. Keep in contact."

"Yes, sir."

Shark and Scatter continued down the hallway that they had just turned down. Every now and then a light would be on. This made it easier for them to see. They passed a few doors as they moved down the hallway and each and every time Shark would silently try the door to see if it would open. Each and every time it was locked, so they moved on. They had not found an open door yet. Soon they came to the end of the hallway and stopped. The hallway merged with a set of stairs that went down. This set of stairs had to have led to the basement only because there was no corresponding "up" stairs to reach a higher level. Shark leaned his head forward and listened. He heard small noises coming from below. Shark pointed to his ear and then pointed to Scatter. Scatter nodded in agreement. He had heard them too.

Shark gave the signal to follow and he slowly made his way down the stairs. Scatter clutched his shotgun and followed. After slowly creeping down 4 flights of stairs, Shark and Scatter had made it to the bottom. They stopped and looked on. Another hallway graced them and they could see more lights on. Just as Shark was about to move forward someone stepped out into the hallway. Shark froze. Scatter didn't move. The individual was coming closer to them and it didn't look like they were going to stop. Shark quickly looked around and noticed that they did not have anywhere to hide. He slowly brought his M4 up and readied it. Right then the person coming at them looked up. He tried to go for his gun but Shark was already ready. He fired and the person in the hall dropped to the ground.

Shark and Scatter moved forward and looked at the body. It was a young woman with a lab-coat on. She had her hand around a pistol and blood was flowing from her head to the floor. She did not have a walkie-talkie. Upset, Shark once again gave the signal to move forward and they advanced. The rest of the team in this lab had to have heard that gunshot. They would probably be coming any minute. He quickly had Scatter go to the other side of the hallway. With them spread out slightly it would be much more difficult for the enemy to hit both of them. Shark and Scatter soon heard stomping feet and a lot of talking. They both took a knee and prepared themselves. They had stopped right before the hallway where the woman had come out. The noises were coming from the down the hallway on the right. The noises were getting louder and Shark knew they were almost on top of them. A moment later a group of three men popped out of the hallway. They were moving fast and they did not expect to see anyone in the hallway. They came around the corner and had no chance. Shark popped off a few rounds and took out one guy. Scatter dropped the other two with a few shells.

They kneeled for a moment longer listening. They didn't hear any more noises so they both stood up and Shark led them down the hallway. Here they saw a few more doors, locked of course, and one set of doors at the end of the hallway. They approached the last set of doors and noticed that they were sealable doors.

"This must be the lab," said Shark to Scatter. Scatter nodded

"We copy as well," said Wire. "Are you ok? We thought we heard gunshots."

"We're fine. Came across four enemies. Target not in sight. We're going into the lab now."

"Copy," said Wire.

Wire had stopped to talk to Shark after she had heard they found the lab. After she was done, she and 8 kept moving. They were in a stairwell that only went up. There was no corresponding "down" stairs. They thought they had heard gunshots from the other way but they were really muffled. Wire and 8 had yet to encounter anyone. They continued to silently move up the stairs. After two flights they were at the top of the landing. Another hallway spread out before them and several doors were present. Wire motioned for 8 to follow and they checked every door they went past. They did not find one that was open. At the end of the hallway, another small hallway turned to the left. It stopped after about ten feet. They both approached the door where a sign stated that the roof was beyond.

"Ghost, Wire. Over."

"Go ahead Wire."

"Ghost it looks like we found the door to the roof. Do you see it?"

"Yeah, I copy. Two enemies already taken care of. There are a few places to hide up there so watch yourself."

"Copy Ghost, watch our ass."

"Copy, over and out."

Wire motioned for 8 and they advanced up the stairs. Surprisingly this was the only door that was unlocked. Wire figured the guys on the roof got there somehow. Fourteen steps later they reached the door that gave access to the roof. Wire knelt down and slowly opened it. 8 took a position above her and scanned the roof as she opened the door.

"Clear," 8 said.

Both Wire and 8 stepped out onto the roof. Ghost was right. There were several places to hide. Ghost wouldn't be able to hit some-one hiding in these places. Wire motioned for 8 to move right. She went left. The first two places were flushed out. No one was there. They both continued their route and flushed out another two places. One last place to hide was at the end of the rook. They continued and converged on the same place. It was also empty. Now, though, Wire and 8 could see two bodies lying limp on the roof. Wire turned in the general direction of Ghost and gave him a thumbs up.

"You're welcome," Ghost said. Suddenly a gunshot rocked the quiet night. Both 8 and Wire turned on instinct. Now, right before them, was a dead body.

"You're welcome for that, too," said Ghost.

Once again Wire looked in Ghost's direction. She flipped him the bird and then said, "Thanks."

"Wi...d...c.py?"

Wire heard the earpiece crackle. "This is Wire. Go ahead," she said.

"Ca…y…he…e?"

"Shark, this is Wire. Do you copy?"

Suddenly there was nothing but silence. "Ghost do you copy?"

"Loud and clear boss," was the response

"Shark and Scatter must have gone into the lab. I'm sure if it was built to contain a pathogen then it surely can mess with our signal. Ghost, 8 and I are heading back down. We are going to meet up with Shark and Scatter."

"Copy," said Ghost.

Shark and Scatter entered the lab cautiously. After they opened the door. They scanned the room and found no one. The lights were on but no one was home. Suddenly something felt wrong to Shark. They had only encountered four enemies in a building engineering a virus. They hadn't even seen the target.

"Spread out," said Shark to Scatter. Scatter nodded and went left. Shark pushed right. The lab was a good size but not huge. They could cover it in less than five minutes. They did so and found no one.

"Wire do you copy?" asked Shark.

"He waited a moment and then said, "Can you hear me?"

The earpiece was silent. Shark looked around. It must be the lab. It was made to ensure nothing biological escaped. It must be messing with the radio transmission.

"Damn it!" said Shark. "It looks like they left before we got here." After looking around the lab some more they could tell that some equipment, as well as supplies, were missing. Suddenly they heard noises coming from outside the lab. They both fell into position behind a table. They readied their weapons and waited. Slowly the lab door creaked open. The muzzle of an M4 peeked through and then Wire advanced. Shark sighed and then put his weapon down. Staying behind the table he yelled out to Wire.

"Wire! It's Shark. We're ok. We're behind the tables. Lower your weapon."

Wire initially tensed when she heard the voice speak. Then, realizing who the voice was and what it was saying, she and 8 lowered their weapons. Shark and Scatter stood out from behind the tables and all four of them advanced to the center of the lab.

"Did you see anyone?" asked Shark.

"No one alive," answered Wire.

Waving his hand across the room Shark said, "It looks like we missed them. I didn't find a small silver case at all."

"Can we get Intel in here to see if they can pick anything up? Maybe a chemist or biologist too?" asked Wire.

"That's exactly what we are going to do. Our mission is over. We failed to capture either target but maybe we can glean something from this lab. Hopefully, they were sloppy."

"Copy that, sir," said Wire. Turning to 8 and Scatter, Wire said, "Head out gentlemen. Let's get out of this building, pick up Ghost, and head back to the rendezvous point."

Both nodded affirmative and brought their weapons to the ready. They started out the door, leading the way. As they came out of the basement, Shark tried the comms again.

"Ghost, Shark. You copy?"

"This is Ghost. I copy."

"Ghost, meet us where we last left you. Mission is over."

"Copy that, sir."

23

Before they had made it to the rendezvous point, Shark had called in to the FOB and relayed status. They would need to be picked up. By the time they had made it back to the rendezvous point, a truck was waiting. They loaded up and rode back to the FOB. The whole ride back Shark thought about their situation. The entire time they were in the building they saw maybe seven enemies and three of those were on the roof. Ghost took care of them. The other four were inside just outside of the lab. Now, with something as precious and valuable as what was in the silver case, Shark figured they would have encountered half an army. With only seven, he wondered what was behind them being there. It was obvious that the main contention had split. But why then keep a few fighters around? The few that they had encountered in the basement even looked surprised to see anyone there. Shark knew he was missing something but could not quite put his finger on it.

After a bumpy, thoughtful ride, they finally pulled up to the gate. The guard let them in and the truck immediately veered for the armory. The truck stopped and everyone piled out. The driver jumped out and spoke to Shark.

"Colonel wants to see all of you in the Fighter Room. He says that you need to check your weapons back in and then meet him there. I am to call him and let him know you are back."

Shark nodded in response and turned to the team.

"Fall-in team," he said. "Let's drop off our weapons and meet the Colonel. Follow me."

Shark led the way into the armory. His team followed. They met the armory guard and followed him back to the spot where he first handed out their equipment. Slowly but surely they doffed their equipment and weapons and handed it back to the guard. One at a time he entered the items back into the cache. After they were done they headed outside. Shark pulled Wire aside.

"Hey Wire. Nice job out there. I know we failed the mission but make sure the team knows that they did a good job. Also, the Colonel wants to see us in the Fighter Room. Do you know where that is?"

"Yes, sir. If it's okay with you I can lead us there."

"Of course. By all means." Shark smiled and bowed slightly. He waved his hands in a gesture for her to lead. Wire chuckled and fell into place at the front of the team.

Wire had led the team to a building that Shark had never been to before. This had not been on the quick tour that he received when he showed up. She led them through the front door and through the main lobby. Connected to the main lobby was a long hallway. They walked about halfway down the hallway and then came to a set of elevators. Wire called an elevator and it came quickly. All of them boarded and Wire hit the button marked B2. The elevator doors closed and the elevator swiftly went down. Soon they re-opened and wire stepped out. The team followed as Wire made a left and walked about twenty feet down the hallway. Wire stepped up to a door on the right and stopped.

"Here we are, sir. After you," she said. Shark stepped up and opened the door.

The team entered a large room meant to hold briefings. Right then it occurred to Shark that this was probably the room where his team received their brief a few days ago. In the middle of the room was a large, smooth table. In the back was a small room with a window in the wall. This room was used to operate the computer, projectors, and projector screens. On the front wall were two large screens. The projectors for these screens were hanging from the ceiling. Colonel Harris was at the head of the table at the back of the room. He stood as the team entered.

"Welcome back, team. Please take a seat," the Colonel said.

Everyone filed in and found a spot. They sat as close as they could in the seats that were next to the Colonel. Wire sat in the seat next to the Colonel on his right and Shark took the seat next to the Colonel's left. As soon as everyone was seated the Colonel spoke. He immediately got to the point.

"I know the mission was a failure. However, I do not believe that it was completely unsuccessful. Granted we did not get either target but we do have an opportunity to scrounge and see what we can acquire. I do not believe that the individual that we are dealing with would be so stupid as to leave anything behind. But, then again, why were there people there then? We believe that they were there to act as some kind of message. Something that the target wanted to relay to us. As they have all been shot we cannot ask any of them."

The Colonel looked around at every team member. They were watching him intently. He continued

"But that's okay. We are sending a team out to the building to gather Intel. We'll get whatever we can, analyze it, and then make a tactical decision from there. Anything further Agent Johns?"

Johns almost forgot his own name. He almost didn't realize that the Colonel was talking to him. He had been so wrapped up in his nickname from the crew that his own name didn't register right away. After a few seconds it clicked, and Johns spoke.

"First, sir, I wanted to report that every person on the team did a fantastic job. They were professional and they knew their job well. Second, and I was thinking about this on the way back to the FOB, I agree with you that something seems off. Why leave people around if you know you are leaving? The target had to have expected us. That's the only thing I can think of. The enemies we encountered seemed shocked to even see us there. Maybe they didn't even know we were coming and the target left them behind to do some sort of task, knowing that they would not make it. Whatever the case is, I do believe that something is not right."

The Colonel had a look on his face like he was considering what Johns had said. It wasn't a look like he was in deep thought but something more like he had already thought of this scenario and was happy that Johns came to the same conclusion.

His head slowly nodded and then it stopped. He looked at the rest of the team.

"Anyone else have anything they want to share?"

No one spoke or volunteered anything so the Colonel spoke up again.

"Okay then. You guys did a good job out there. We may not have gotten what we wanted but we didn't lose anybody and that's just as important. I have personally spoken to each and every one of your supervisors and they agree that all of you are now on leave. For two weeks. Vacation if you are a civilian." Colonel Harris looked at 8.

"If you think of something else about this mission you can call me back. I will give all of you my contact information. If nothing comes to mind then I want you to enjoy your time off."

The Colonel started to stand and everyone around the table beat him to it.

"Carry on," said the Colonel and everyone relaxed.

24

Johns and his team stood together in the airport. Before they boarded the plane they all swapped contact information. Contacts were always great to have and the contacts you previously worked with were the best kind. When they were done they all walked together to their gate. They were all boarding the same plane as they were all going back to the United States. They said their goodbyes early in case they would not see each other again. They boarded and soon found out that, indeed, their seats were not next to each other. The plane flight was very long but pretty much uneventful.

Towards the end of the flight, Johns noticed that Wire, now Amanda, had an empty seat next to her. He decided he was going to join her and try to engage in small talk. Anything to help continue to pass the time. He unbuckled his seatbelt and stood. He politely said excuse me to the person next to him and shuffled past until he was in the aisle. He made his way over to Amanda and sat down. She was reading a book and set it down in her lap when he sat next to her.

"Whatcha reading?" Johns asked.

Amanda smiled and said, "*Riverworld,* by Philip Jose Farmer. I really enjoyed *The World of Tiers* so I figured I would give this a try. I am on the last book in this series and I am a little disappointed. I was hoping for something a little better."

Johns asked, "Better? Like how?"

"Well, it just seemed to me like he had a really good idea. He got a few books out of it and then the rest were just to string along this idea. To a point, he stretched the idea too thin by making the journey take too long. The people not from Earth were his deus ex machina. They were godlike and so almost anything could happen. Again, interesting story I just preferred *Tiers* better."

"Did you read *Dayworld* yet?" asked Johns.

"Well, well, Agent Johns. You read Sci-fi?"

"Some. I like a little bit of everything. Sci-fi, fantasy, action, adventure, horror. Oh, but no sparkling vampires. My kind of vampire is tough and hates sunlight."

Amanda giggled and Johns smiled.

"So how has your flight been so far?" asked Amanda.

"Pretty boring. I don't have a book on me. I should have brought one but I didn't. I have slept most of the way so I guess that's something."

"Very impressive. Most people can barely even close their eyes on a plane let alone sleep."

"I have been able to sleep on planes for as long as I can remember. I can fold the tray down and then bend over and lay my head down. Of course, because I am bent over like that for an extended period of time, my legs fall asleep. But hell, the prices we pay."

Both of them laughed now. They both could tell the other was enjoying the conversation. Suddenly Amanda started coughing. At first, it was a few small coughs. It turned to larger and longer ones and Amanda reached for the napkin she received with her drink. She covered her mouth and wiped with her napkin. When she pulled it away blood was smeared on it and the corner of her mouth.

"Are you okay?" asked Johns.

"Excuse me," was all she said. He moved out of the way as she was unbuckling her seat belt. She passed him and headed for the bathroom. She was in the bathroom for about ten minutes before she finally returned. Johns once again moved out of the way and she sat back down. She buckled her belt and looked at Johns.

"I'll be okay. Must be catching a cold or something."

Johns spoke up. "Most people don't spit blood with the common cold. Are you sure you're okay?"

She smiled at him. "I'll be fine. I'll stop at the drug store when I get back and pick up some medicine. I'll start taking it early. Maybe this thing won't last very long."

Right then the *Buckle Your Seatbelt* sign came on followed by the captain speaking over the intercom.

"Hello, folks. This is your captain speaking. When are getting close to Hartsfield-Jackson International in Atlanta and we are going to start prepping for landing. We have about another forty-five minutes before we have wheels on the ground. In that time please help the stewardess' in gathering up your trash and putting your trays in the upright position. We will have landing data for you once we get a little closer. Again, if you need assistance with anything please let us know. Thank you."

The intercom hung up and the stewardess's started to shuffle about. Johns spoke again to Amanda.

"Well, I need to get back to my seat but let me know if you need anything. And please, see a doctor when we get back."

Amanda smiled and nodded and Johns stood up. He walked back over to his seat, sat down, and buckled up.

Soon the plane was landing and taxiing to the gate. As soon as they made it to the gate everyone started to shuffle off the plane. Johns grabbed his gear from the overhead and followed the crowd. He exited the plane and walked up the ramp to the airport proper. He would miss the team he worked with but a vacation would also be nice. He had not packed more than what he carried on board with him and so he didn't need to stop at baggage claim. He headed for long-term parking to grab his car. When he got to his car he slumped down into the driver's side and rested his head back on the seat.

'Finally home,' he thought. 'Time to relax.'

Johns started the car and drove out of the parking lot. He drove out through the exit lanes and stopped at the parking booth. He paid his parking fees and the gate came up. He drove past and merged with traffic to exit the airport. Once on the lanes that left the airport, Johns would have a little bit of a drive to get home. He flipped on the radio and sat silently while he drove towards his house.

25

Johns landed in Las Vegas a day later. He was going to take his time off seriously. In other words, he wasn't going to think about work at all. A few drinks and some gambling were things he had in mind when he booked the tickets. He made it home from his flight back from Tehran and the idea just seemed to come to him. He would probably see a show or two but this time off was meant to be non-stressful. He wasn't going to make any huge decisions; just take the chips as they might fall. The thought of chips made John slightly hungry to play Poker. Maybe he could mix in a little Blackjack.

He got a taxi and left the airport. The taxi took him to his hotel and he checked in. A bellhop took his bags and showed him to his room. The bellhop opened the door and escorted Johns in. He set the bags down gently and explained what Johns could expect from the concierge service. He talked to him about room service and the maid service. When he was done he stood for a minute in front of Johns. Johns took that as his cue and pulled out a few dollars for his tip. The bellhop grabbed the money and left, closing the door behind him. Johns stood at the foot of the bed looking around the room.

This is going to be a good week, thought Johns. He turned and fell backward onto the bed. He more or less bounced rather than sinking into the mattress.

"Same ol' mattress no matter where you go," said Johns out loud. He chuckled slightly at the absurdity of the hotel mattress. He was debating on what to do first when it occurred to him.

Take a shower, said a voice in his head. He sniffed his armpits and reeled. He wasn't that bad but the flight from Atlanta to Vegas was a little long. Not as long as the one from Tehran to Atlanta but long enough. He decided to freshen up first and then hit the town. It was still light out and the craziness would not have started yet anyway. He freshened up via way of the shower and brushing his teeth. He decided he would start with a show. He wanted to hit up the poker players a little into the night. That way they had enough time to drink a few before he got to the table. After that they were easy prey; donkeys, some would call them.

The show was very exciting indeed. It was a group of guys who performed using black-lights. They would wear different colored clothing and use different colored equipment. Based on the color of their clothing and equipment you would only see want they wanted you to see. At times it looked like they were floating or flying. At other times it looked like they were throwing each other across the room. Their props and equipment also seemed to take on these same properties. They seemingly told a story with each act but Johns was way too mesmerized by the stunts to care what story they were telling.

After the show, Johns walked out of the theater and saw that the sun had set. He rubbed his hands together like a greedy child and spoke only to himself. "Here we go," he whispered. Johns walked to the nearest casino and entered through the large double doors. This set of double doors opened into the lobby of the casino's hotel. It was purposefully set up this way because then you had to walk down the long hallway that passed by shop after shop. Only then would you reach the gambling area. Johns sighed and walked through the doors. He headed down the hallway and noticed that the floors were all marble. It was beautiful and Johns thought, *Wow, a lot of people have to be losing to afford this.* He continued on and passed in front of a chocolate shop. He stopped immediately. Johns was not going to buy any candy but what had caught his attention was what was in the shop. Starting from the ceiling and working its way down to the floor was one giant chocolate fountain. This fountain did not go straight down, oh no, it curved and twisted and flowed through most of the front of the shop. Johns felt like such a kid watching it but it was quite interesting as he had never seen one that big before.

After a few minutes of watching the chocolate flow, he moved on. He passed a few more shops with things that he was not going to buy. Maybe at the end of his vacation he would get a souvenir. For now, however, the money he would win would make up for not buying a souvenir. Today was day one and so he was going to start off with small stakes and see where that got him. If he won he would move on to higher stakes if it looked like luck was on his side. If not, he could easily stay with the small stakes and have fun. He entered the gambling floor and it opened up. Walking through the smaller hallway did not prepare you for entering the gambling floor. It was gargantuan. There was only one floor for this casino and because of that, it was spread out. Slot machines were everywhere. To the left were table games. He would find Blackjack in that direction. Turning his head clockwise he could see in the back of the room was the Sports betting area. There were large TVs set up with every kind of sport you could imagine. There was a large digital display on the wall and numbers and names flew by.

Further to the right was where the poker room would be. He would head over there tonight. If he had to cooldown he could head over to Blackjack for a while; slow his betting down if need be. Right in the middle of the floor was the Craps tables. They were full. Johns had tried to watch Craps several times to learn it. It looked like you could win money, and he often heard people state how they did, but it never sunk in for him and so he never learned. He always thought there was too much going on with Craps for him to keep straight. He gave the room one last look and headed over to the Poker tables.

Johns woke up at 1030 when his phone beeped at him that he had a missed call. The light stabbed his eyes as he tried to open them and he suddenly remembered last night. Granted he had had a few drinks but those around him were more inebriated. His headache would go away after he drank some water and took a shower. He reached for his phone and knocked it on the floor.

"Damn it!" he said to no one. Johns shuffled the comforter off of him and swung his legs out of bed. He found where his phone had bounced to when he knocked it off of the end table. He picked it up and looked at his missed calls. He must have really been out of it because he had three missed calls! He didn't recognize the number right away but it was the same for all three calls. His phone said he had three messages. He held the number one key down to get his voicemail. He put in his PIN and waited. After listening to all three voicemails carefully, he listened to them again. After the last voicemail had ended, Johns was completely awake. He couldn't believe who had called him and what they had said.

26

Johns had his stuff packed and was down in the lobby checking out early. *So much for a rousing vacation,* thought Johns. After listening to his voicemails he had called the person who left them. It looked like he was headed back to Atlanta. He was now to be part of a study being performed by the CDC. It seems that two of his previous team members, Amanda and Thomas, had just died. He told the CDC about how one of them had coughed up blood but had otherwise felt fine. Johns had not seen the other one when they got off of the plane. Johns gave them a report on his health, and other than a headache gotten from having a good time, he felt fine. No blood had come out of any of his orifices. The CDC had deemed him healthy for travel and had requested his immediate attendance at the CDC.

After he had hung up the phone he gave his boss a quick call. Agent Walsh and been informed already about what was going on and was on the same page with the CDC. Johns acknowledged this from his boss and he promised her that he would be there on the first flight out. Walsh told him that she would use her connections to get his flight from a few days from now changed to a flight that left very soon. He hung up the phone and flew into a frenzy with packing his bags. This only exacerbated his headache but that couldn't be helped.

After checking out Johns was soon in a taxi heading to the airport. After a not so quick flight back to Atlanta, the CDC had a driver waiting for him just outside baggage claim. Johns found the sign with his name on it, was ushered quickly into a limo and was soon heading back to the place where his journey had started. In the back seat of the limo was a medical mask for Johns to wear. He put it on. Johns made his way through the CDC and found the lab. Dr. Boone was set up and had been waiting for him. Boone had been given this case because he had been involved with it from the beginning. Johns was walking through the lab doors when Boone immediately started talking.

"Welcome back, Agent Johns. Sorry, it was under these conditions and I am truly sorry for having ruined your vacation."

"Can I see them?" asked Johns.

Boone stared at Johns. He was obviously anxious and possibly scared.

"Well…." stammered Boone.

"Don't give me that bullshit. Let me see them."

Knowing that he shouldn't Boone gave in.

"Follow me," Boone said.

Boone took the lead and led Johns to the morgue. This morgue was different than most morgues in that it was hermetically sealed to prevent the escape of potential contaminants from organic specimens. After getting the proper attire on and going through the decontamination chamber, Boone opened the door to the morgue. He walked Johns over to two tables that had bodies on them. The bodies were covered with sheets and bare feet stuck out of the sheets at the bottom of the table. The big toe of each body had an identification tag on it. As Boone uncovered both bodies Johns spoke.

"How did they acquire the virus?"

"We're not sure. We believe that at some point when you were in Tehran you were subjected to it."

"That doesn't make sense," Johns pleaded. "Not one of us was injected with anything. We didn't get hit or shot or stabbed."

Boone gestured towards the bodies and Johns looked. Suddenly, the mask Johns had on his face seemed not tight enough. Both bodies looked exactly like the body of the driver that had crashed in front of the Taylor's house. However, that driver had been black and both Amanda and Thomas were white. Johns announced that fact to Boone.

"We noticed that too," said Boone. "That can only mean that the virus that was originally created has been modified for several different levels of melanin. Now I don't believe that that is the surprising part. We knew what was in the silver case when you caught the creator. What surprises me is the same thing that concerns you. Not one of you was poked, prodded, or stabbed with anything. So how did they come down with the virus? Also, Agent, you're white. Why are you not sick?"

Johns stared at Boone for a minute. He was dumbfounded. Why wasn't he sick? And how did they come across the virus? It suddenly hit him.

"The virus is airborne now," said Johns, wide-eyed and staring at Boone.

Boone shook his head up and down very slowly. It was an ominous head shake and it suddenly sunk in for Johns what the implications were.

"We all left for vacation after the mission. They could have come into contact with lots of people. Those people then could have come into contact with lots of people. This could turn out to be very bad."

"Agreed," said Boone. "Before you got here we were getting calls about really sick people. Same symptoms as these bodies and the one you saw at the Taylor's house. Hospitals were the ones calling us and its only getting worse. And guess what? Only white people are filling the beds. The hospitals didn't say it like that but I asked and they confirmed. Some things are starting to add up and they're not good.

"Like?" asked Johns.

"Like when we had the Taylors in here and we realized they weren't infected. The man in their front yard had been black and they were white. They may have contracted the virus, although I don't think they did, but it would not have affected them. Even at that time though we don't believe that the virus had been engineered for air dispersion. The case was still recently stolen and there wasn't any evidence that it had been altered to survive in that form. However, after talking to Agent Walsh, she was able to get me some info on what was found in the lab in Tehran. I believe the air dispersion conversion was accomplished there. Your team probably came into contact with it when you went into either the building itself or the lab."

Boone was still looking at Johns while he talked. Johns was seemingly looking off into space.

"Agent, you still with me?" Boone asked as he snapped his fingers in the air. Johns came out of his own head and spoke.

"I was just trying to think of when that could have been. I don't remember getting sprayed or anything.' Suddenly Johns' eyes got bigger.

"The team did split up at one point. Both Amanda and Thomas went one way. I went the other. Could they have been sprayed then?"

"It's likely," said Boone. "You still came in contact with them afterward."

They both stood staring at each other for a moment.

"So what do we need to do now doctor?" asked Johns.

"Remember the tests I had to perform on the Taylors?" asked Boone. Johns shook his head.

"I will have to do the same on you. And, I will have to keep you in the same room that they were in. When we called you in Vegas we did not know at the time that the virus was transmittable by air. We left the mask you have on now on the backseat of the limo just in case. It turns out that might have been a good move. At the least for the staff here at the CDC. Unfortunately, because we couldn't get to you quickly, everyone you came in contact with may have caught the virus."

Johns was taken aback. He hoped that he would not be partly responsible for killing people like this. If he *had* been infected then he did not think that it could be avoided that he infected others. His heart sank.

"What about the other two on the team?" asked Johns.

"They have been contacted and they seem healthy and fine. They were asked to come in for tests and it seems they do not have the virus. We have their blood work and are constantly performing the same series of tests that you are about to receive. They are still here. They are in the room next to yours. Because they are healthy we believe that the virus that your team was exposed to was a strain that affected the level of melanin only seen in white people. Obviously, the twins are black. This could be good news. Maybe the strain that affects that level of melanin has not been released. Regardless, we still need to test you."

Johns nodded. He remembered the process from when the Taylors were in the same room he was about to be put in.

"Listen, Agent Johns," Boone started. "I would like to start your process as soon as we can. If this virus did get out to the population, and I believe it did, we need to try to work on some sort of cure. This virus works very fast as we have already seen. With hospitals filling up we need to have some sort of answer. Right now were are working on it but we are basically tied down, metaphorically speaking, because we do not have enough data. Maybe you are that last piece of data we need. Time is our enemy, Agent."

After that speech, Johns stared at Boone. If it was true he may be some sort of missing link. Some needed piece of data that could help save thousands or even millions of lives. He could withstand a few pokes and prods for that to be accomplished.

"Okay," Johns said. "Lead the way Doc."

Boone smiled and covered up the bodies on both tables. He headed for the decontamination room and shut the door. After the process was complete he opened the first door and they both walked out into the prep room. They doffed their attire and put it into a waste-basket for clothing. Everything went into the basket except the mask Johns was wearing. He had to keep that on until the tests came back with some sort of result. Boone then led Johns out of the morgue and down the hallway towards the elevator. The elevator trip was short and soon they were on the floor that was recognizable by Johns. This was the same floor he had walked the Taylors down. They left the elevator and made it to the door to his room. Boone swiped his badge and the door unlocked. Johns knew the routine and he followed Boone into the room. Johns shut the door behind him and walked over to the second door to the second room. Boone was standing by the computer and once again punching buttons. The second room door unlocked and Boone opened it. He stepped in and shut it behind him. Quickly the glass wall became transparent and Johns heard the microphone click on.

"Okay Agent I know you know the drill but I want you to know that I will make this as painless and as quick as I can. I am going to get my supplies and then I will be back down to draw your blood.

That is our first step and then I will walk you through everything else from there."

Johns nodded and smiled. He said, "While you're doing that can you order some food? I'm hungry."

Boone grinned and chuckled slightly. "Of course," he said.

27

Boone was back in no time and he had grabbed his supplies. This time he had an assistant with him, however, to help him with the door controls. He went over to the lockers in the corner and donned his full suit. After all, he was white as well and if Johns had the virus he could catch it. His assistant sat down at the computer and found the button to unlock the door. The glass was still transparent so she didn't have to adjust that. Boone finished and walked over to the door to Johns' room. He looked back at his assistant and nodded. The assistant hit the button on the screen and unlocked the door. It clicked and Boone opened it and walked in. He shut the door behind him and walked over to the bed. The assistant ensured that the button for the gas was pulled up and within view.

"Please sit Agent Johns," said Boone.

Johns did as he was told. He had decided he was not going to fight anything. Why would he? He wanted to help people; especially if he was the cause of the deaths. Boone set down a small case on the bed and started pulling out equipment. He set them on the bed in the order they would be used. As Boone started the process it made Johns' memory flashback to when the Taylors were here. It was a bit of déjà vu as this same thing had happened to them. Johns knew pretty much everything that was going on so he would not request to be updated like they did. He just hoped they would keep the food coming. Johns chuckled slightly at this thought and his body jumped a little.

"Hold still, Agent. I am almost done," said Boone. "I need a few vials for the various tests."

"Sorry," said Johns.

"Out of curiosity, what was so funny?"

"Oh it wasn't much," said Johns. "I was thinking about when the Taylors were here and how I am now in their same shoes. I plan on doing anything and everything you ask but the one thing I was hoping for was that you just keep the food coming."

They both smiled at each other.

"I will keep you as safe and healthy as possible. The same promise I made to the Taylors."

"I know," said Johns.

Boone pulled out the needle and put a cotton swab and Band-Aid over the puncture on Johns' skin. Boone began wrapping up his supplies and putting them back into his case. He finished, stood, and walked towards the door. He turned back to Johns and spoke.

"I'll let you know what I find."

Johns nodded. Boone looked at his assistant and gave the signal. His assistant unlocked the door and it clicked. Boone opened it and went through. He shut the door and walked over to the computer desk. Johns heard the microphone click on and Boone grabbed it to talk. "Agent Johns I am going to leave now and we have to darken the glass. I will ensure someone keeps an eye on you in case you need anything. This may be a long process, several days at least, so try to relax. When your food comes, if you would like anything like a book or something, just let them know."

Johns gave Boone a thumbs up as the glass was going dark. Before it got too dark Johns saw the front door open and it looked like someone was coming in with a tray of food. *Thank god,* thought Johns. Soon the smaller door, inside of his larger door, opened. The food tray slid in and he grabbed it. He gobbled everything down and took the cup they provided and drank some water he ran from the sink in the bathroom. After he was done he slid the tray back next to the door. He went back over to the bed to lie down. He figured he wouldn't be able to sleep at all with everything going on. He was wrong. Soon he was out.

28

It sucked spending time in this room. Johns was bored out of his mind. It had only been three days but he was already out of ideas on how to keep himself occupied. He had requested a few books and he had gotten them. He started to read but soon found out that he still needed to get out and do something. Obviously, with that not being an option, he tried to read some more. His mind would start to wander and then he would get restless again. The food came on a regular basis and that helped him keep some sanity. He was beginning to understand the Taylors' point of view.

Boone would come in every now and then and give him an update. That was nice too but it was unpredictable. It was sporadic enough that it was tearing at the fringe of the sanity that Johns was trying to maintain. On the second day, Walsh had come to see him. They talked for a little while, another distractor from losing his mind, and Walsh promised to buy him a beer when he got out. She brought him disturbing news of increased reports of sick people. The hospitals were full and people were dying in their homes. It seemed the virus had spread and spread quickly. However, the virus that Johns' team had been subjected to was not the only one out there. Other races were seemingly dropping dead. Once contracted the virus acted quickly. It produced the sores and boils on the skin and then swiftly killed the person. Johns had seen this several times, first hand, and it was not pretty.

With other races now dropping left and right, Johns was not so sure that a cure could be found. Maybe his blood could lead to something but would that still work for someone who was not white? There were reports of other people like him but they were few and far between. The visits to him were getting slimmer, although the food kept coming. The talks were also limited and the last one he had had with Boone was interesting. Boone seemed like he had a cold. Johns saw the real signs. Boone displayed the same demeanor that Amanda did when Johns had talked to her on the plane to Atlanta. Boone had wiped his mouth and Johns had seen blood on the tissue.

"You okay?" asked Johns.

Boone spoke into the microphone. "I'm alright. I feel like I have a cold. My head hurts all the time."

Johns spoke. "You know what you have."

"I know, but I am trying everything I can to find a cure. I haven't found anything yet and it is literally killing me."

Boone tried to smile but Johns could tell it hurt to do it. Boone kept talking.

"I did find some similarities between your blood and others I tested. While I was testing your blood I learned that you were O-. I recalled someone else's blood that I recently saw that was the same type. Actually two people. The Taylors. Both of them had O- blood type. I haven't really been coming to see you lately because I feel like there is a connection with blood type so I have diligently been working on that."

Boone coughed and some blood missed the tissue and it landed on the floor. He tried to wipe it up with the tissue in his hand but instead ended up smearing more on the floor.

"Damn it," he whispered. Boone walked over to the lockers and pulled out a medical rag and a spray bottle with some kind of disinfectant. He walked back over to the smeared blood and sprayed whatever was in the bottle on it. He wiped up the blood with the new rag. When he was done he put the spray bottle back and discarded the rag into the bin next to the lockers. When he got back to his chair he plopped down in it. Johns spoke.

"So you think that there is a way to stop this virus based off of blood type? Specifically O-?"

"Yes, I do. The virus attacks a person based off of the amount of melanin produced by the body. In other words, skin color. This melanin is carried through the blood and deposited where needed. If, for some reason, O- blood does not allow the spread of the virus maybe there is something there to try to create a cure. Maybe O- just captures the virus and doesn't let it go. I really am not sure because I have yet to try it. We have been losing people to this virus left and right and even though I am working on this issue as much as I can I am only one person."

Boone looked at Johns with pleading eyes. They were droopy and sad. Johns immediately felt responsible. He knew that in reality, it was a damn terrorist that had unleashed this plague. But he still couldn't help but feel responsible for helping to spread the virus. He even gave the virus the ultimate way to not only escape from isolation but the fastest way to spread around the world: a ride on an airplane. Boone spoke again breaking Johns from his thoughts.

"I am going to get back to the lab for now. This virus is quick acting and I want to try to get something more done on trying to create a cure before I die. My wife and kids are already gone so I don't have much to go home to anyway. I might as well stay here and work. Maybe someone will find my work, finish it, and then give out the cure."

Boone stood and Johns stood with him. Boone walked towards the door and then turned slightly.

"I will be back for you. I am going to leave the glass transparent and the microphone on so we don't have to mess with the computer anymore."

He turned back around and walked through the door. Johns put his hand on the glass in a sad gesture of hope. He hoped he would see the doctor again.

29

Another twelve hours had passed and Johns hadn't talked to anyone. The food had stopped coming and he was hungry. In the Army, he had gone longer than this without food and he knew he could do it. That did not stop his stomach from growling, however. Johns thought about the situation he was in and he began to worry. If everyone was dead at the CDC who would be able to let him out of this room? Would he ever get out or would he die in here? Maybe dying in here was karma coming back to bite his ass. Maybe he deserved to die in here. He slumped down in front of the bed and put his head in his hands. He didn't really have any family so he couldn't miss them. The one person he thought of right now, actually, was Walsh. She was his boss but he had feelings for her. He never told her but he thought maybe she liked him too. They never did anything about it because of their superior-to-subordinate situation. It seemed like to him though, that at times, they had flirted. Maybe that was all in his dying head. He did know that she didn't have a family either. She had been married once but that was definitely over. He decided that if he had one dying wish it would be to tell her how he felt. At that moment Johns heard the door open to the computer room. He couldn't see anyone because he was still on the floor and the glass didn't go that low. He heard the door, however, because the microphone was still on. Or was he hearing things? Maybe he was going crazy. Knowing you may be the only one left can really mess with your mind.

Johns decided to look anyway. He stood up and looked out the glass. Immediately he saw Boone lying halfway in the room. It looked like he had opened the door and then fell into the room, unable to get up. His body was halfway in the room and halfway in the hallway. His face was destroyed with sores and boils. Blood was running out of the sores and starting to run out of his mouth. It was now coating the floor around his head. He tried one last movement and all that he could do was stretch out his left arm. It poked into the room and then fell flat on the ground. Boone didn't move again. Johns could see that there was a piece of paper in Boone's left hand. The paper was folded up and it was not big by any means. Johns started to wonder what was written on it. It couldn't have been his research as that would have taken up a lot of paper. Maybe he was trying to get Johns some information about what he found. Again, there couldn't be too much written on the piece of paper. Johns began to worry anew about his situation. He turned to look at the door and started thinking about how to get out.

30

Six hours into it and Johns still had not found a way to get out of his room. He was tired and he had cut his left arm. In the process of receiving that cut, he had also smashed his left hand. Johns was hungry. He hadn't eaten for almost a day now and his fatigue was coming on quicker and quicker. His room was a mess. He had tried to use everything in this room as a tool just to get out. He attempted to use the dresser to try and smash the transparent glass. That was a bust. Literally. The dresser busted into splinters and now it lay scattered on his floor. He tried to examine the door. The door had a smaller door inside, he knew, and he tried to look for the edges. It was seamless. He still had his food tray from his last meal so he attempted to use it like a crowbar. Unfortunately with nothing to stick it into it just slid right off the door. In frustration, he slammed the tray into the door several times. All that did was crumple the tray and make him more tired. After the tray incident, he sat there for a moment getting his breath. Once it was back, he stood. He grabbed his cup and went to the sink in the bathroom. He filled his cup and then took a long draw. Johns was happy the power was still on. Otherwise, not only would he not be able to see to even attempt to get out but the water pumps wouldn't be working either. He would die much quicker.

After his break, he jumped right back into trying to save himself. He left the bathroom and stopped immediately. Something had just occurred to him. If he intentionally made the power shut off would the door unlock? It was worth a try considering nothing else he was doing was working. He walked over to the door and picked up the demolished tray. He was hoping it was stainless steel and not aluminum. Otherwise, his idea was not going to work. He ran back over to his bed and jumped up on it. He was shy of hitting the lights by about two feet. Johns stopped jumping and looked around. He didn't see anything else in his room that could give him a boost. He dropped to the bed and hung his head low. He rolled over and dropped the tray over the side of the bed. He thought more about how he wasn't going to get out of here.

While he was dropping the tray over the side of the bed, his left hand came to rest on the side of the bed. The idea to use the box springs came to him immediately. He jumped up once again and nearly fell over. He started seeing stars and had to hang his head low to just breathe right and regain his sight. This not eating thing was going to get him if he kept up this physical activity. The stars went away and he moved the mattress off of the box springs. He positioned the box spring so it was sitting upright on the wall. There was nothing for him to climb on so he took the mangled tray and stabbed it at the underside of the box springs. The fabric there was thin and it ripped easily. He then ripped the rest of the fabric off and saw the set of springs underneath. These would make perfect steps for when he was climbing up. His plan was to use the box springs like a ladder. Once he was at the top he would use the tray as originally intended. He would smash the light out, which would, unfortunately, make it darker, but it would leave an open space for him to use the tray to short circuit the light.

Johns was hoping that that would cause a power loss that would open the door.

Johns backed up to the other wall and took off running for the box springs. The first time he tried he slipped on the splintered wood from the dresser. He cleared a path for himself the second time and took off running. There wasn't much room to get any kind of speed. He hit the box springs and climbed it like a ladder. Soon he was at the top and hugging the wall. He slowly stood and gained balance at the top. Standing there, hugging the wall, the light was now within reach. He carefully took a few practice swings and realized that he easily could smash the light and get the tray to touch. Finally, he took a swing with as much strength as he had left. Not only did he smash the light but he also got the tray to stick. Unfortunately, he took the shock as well and fell down the box springs. Johns knew he may take a shock but did not expect what he got. As he tumbled down the box springs and towards the floor, one of the springs cut his left arm. As soon as he hit the floor his left hand was under him and his hand got smashed. He bounced off the floor once and hit his head pretty hard. This time the stars didn't go away and he let his head fall to the floor. His eyes slowly closed and his body went limp.

31

Johns slowly opened his eyes. What light remained stabbed them and he closed them again. He scrunched up his face in pain and touched the part of his head that hurt the worst. His hand pulled away with blood. It had stopped, luckily, and so Johns had not bled out. There was only a small pool of blood on the floor. Slowly opening his eyes again Johns took in the light. It dawned on him then that his little trick had not worked. He looked at his watch and saw that he had been out for almost three hours. He looked around. His room was still in shambles and he was nowhere near any closer to getting out. Johns rolled onto his back and just laid there. He tightened and untightened his left hand several times. It hurt but it still worked. While he was doing that he noticed his left arm hurt. He looked at it and then remembered what had happened. Luckily the cut was not too deep. Johns sat up slowly and ripped the bottom piece of his shirt off. With the cloth strip he now had, he tried to tie it around his arm where the cut was. It was difficult but he got it done.

Johns wasn't sure what would happen if he laid back down so he stayed sitting up. He felt like his life was on its last leg. He might have been able to go a little longer without food, but the blood loss had changed that.

If the door was open right now he would have enough energy to get out of this building. But he would not have enough energy anymore to try and claw his way out. Johns slowly scooted towards the glass wall. He leaned against it and slumped low. The glass was just above his head and so his body felt the entire coldness that emitted from the wall. He felt like he was slumped so low that his body was going to meld into itself.

Suddenly a noise came from outside his room. It had come from the other room and he thought it was someone's voice. A female voice, perhaps? Maybe Johns was going crazy. It was finally happening. He was going to die. Then, Johns heard the voice again. He had forgotten the microphone was on. His heart started to beat a little faster. Johns needed to stand up right now. Whoever that was would be able to help him get out. He slowly sat straight up. His head pounded but he ignored it. He forced himself to climb into a kneeling position. From there he grabbed at the wall to steady himself. He was able to get one foot underneath him and he paused for a minute. Passing out now would not do him any good. There it was again, the voice. He could have sworn that the voice shouted his name. Finally, he was able to stand up fully and look out through the transparent glass.

She was like an angel. Johns could have sworn that a light emanated from her. Maybe she was an angel come to take him to heaven. Maybe it was just the bump on his head playing tricks on his vision. He saw the female angel move closer to the microphone. Johns blinked hard and then realized who it was.

"Johns you okay?" asked Walsh.

Johns' eyes started to water. She had come for him. Just when he thought he was going to die, someone that he could love had come for him.

"I'm okay, I guess," he responded. He touched his head again and put his bloody hand on the glass.

"Jesus H. Christ! You're bleeding," she stammered.

"Yeah, I know but I'm fine. Can you get me out of here?"

"That's why I'm here," she said. She smiled and then moved over to the computer desk. It took a moment of her fiddling with the screens but Johns finally heard the door click. He turned toward it and saw out of the corner of his eye, Walsh, running towards it. She made it to the door well before he did and she swung it open. She came in and almost tackled him. At least that's what it felt like to him.

"Oww! Easy, easy," he said.

"Sorry," she said with sympathy in her eyes. She grabbed him around the waist more gently now and led him past the now opened door. She took most of his weight on her shoulders but she let him limp as best he could. They made their way towards the front door and Johns saw Boone once again.

"Wait a sec," Johns said.

"We need to get out of here. Get you some help," insisted Walsh.

"Hold on a minute. Lower me down."

Walsh grumbled and sighed but slowly lowered Johns to the floor. He came down on both knees and sat there a second. Then he reached out for the note in Boone's hand. He grabbed it and his hand brushed against Boone's. He shivered. Boone's hand was ice cold and it burrowed its way even more into Johns' mind that Boone was dead. He took the note and looked at it. He cried slightly and Walsh leaned down to help him up again. He took her help and she stood him up against the wall by the door. She moved through the door, stepping over Boone. Walsh then reached back through the door for Johns. He took her arm and slowly made his way over Boone. Once they had made it to the hallway, the lights went out. They stood there for several moments embracing each other. With a hum and a click, the lights came back on. These lights were different, however. They were the emergency lights and they were on the backup diesel generator power. There was not as many and they were not as bright as the normal lights.

"We need to get out of here," said Walsh.

"I agree," said Johns. They hobbled down the hallway and made a right. The elevators did not run on emergency power and so they would have to take the stairs up. They found the stairs and started up. This was slow going for both of them but they finally made it to the floor they were looking for. They opened the door to the floor and came out. They once again hobbled down the hallway and came to a doorway that was unfamiliar to Johns. Walsh saw the look in his eyes and spoke.

"This is the back entrance. I parked out back so no one would see me. There are not many people left but the ones that are…" She stopped talking.

"It's okay. Let's get out of here," said Johns. They struggled to the back door and opened it. The light was dying outside and they hobbled down the steps and headed towards Walsh's car. Johns had not seen the world for several days now and in that time it had changed. The world must have gone crazy when everyone started dying. Littered everywhere were trash and bodies. Maybe now those two things were the same. Cars were also strewn in places that made it very hard to drive. How Walsh got here was amazing. Maybe that is why it took her so long to get him. She started to tell him, inside the CDC, about the new world but stopped talking. Johns knew he was about to get a crash course in it. They headed for her car and she slumped him against the back door. She unlocked the doors and opened the back.

"I want you to lay down for now. I am going to go back into the CDC and get some supplies. You need to be stitched up and I'll see if I can find some food. You'll be okay here, just stay down and be quiet."

She shuffled him into the back seat and he laid down. She shut the door and locked it. He looked up to see her going back into the CDC. He laid his head back down and almost as soon as his head hit the seat he was out.

32

Johns woke to the sound of the car being shut off. He had bounced in and out of consciousness a few times with the jostling of the car. He knew Walsh was headed somewhere but he didn't know where. It was dark and Johns couldn't tell what time it was. He tried to look at his watch but he was stiff from being in the back seat. He just laid there. Walsh got out of the car and shut her door. She headed over to the back of the car and opened the door.

"Come on Colton," said Walsh. She was reaching into the backseat and taking hold of him. He was trying to move and it was coming along slowly. That was one of the only times she had used his first name. Even with the small amount of flirting they had still always used each other's last names. This thought warmed him and he pushed his body a little harder. With both of them working he was able to get out of the back seat and stand outside the car.

"Thanks, Jenna," he tried. She smiled and kissed him on the cheek. The sudden rush of energy allowed him to hobble alongside her. They were in a garage. Jenna had parked the car in one and shut the door. They walked alongside the car and towards the door that led to the house.

"What if someone is home?" asked Colton.

"They're not," said Jenna. "I already checked. Come on, I need to get you bandaged up."

Colton hung onto Jenna as she opened the door. They passed through it and she shut it behind them. Colton clung to Jenna as she walked him to the kitchen. From there she found the hallway that led to the master bedroom.

"Here, lie down," said Jenna to Colton.

She walked him over to the bed and laid him down.

"Stay here. I need to find a few things."

Jenna went back out to the car and grabbed the bag of medical supplies she got from the CDC. She went back into the house and made her way back to the bedroom. When she went in she saw that Colton had passed out again. She set the supplies down on the dresser next to the bed. She knew he was going to be fine. His wounds were not that severe. The worst that had happened to him was the bump he took to the head. He could have a concussion and that might take a while to overcome. Knowing he was fine she walked to the back door and then the front door. She ensured both doors were locked. She even moved a chair in front of both.

She then went back to the bedroom and grabbed the medical bag. She sat on the bed next to him and started unloading all of the supplies she would need. When she was done unloading the gear she started stitching him up. It didn't take long and when she was done she covered him up with the bed's comforter. She put the bag back on the dresser and then left him to sleep. Jenna made her way back to the car and grabbed the food supplies she nabbed from the CDC. She took them to the kitchen and put them away. So far the power was working at this house and so she utilized the refrigerator. When she opened the door there was more food in there from the previous occupants. Jenna smiled and stuffed what she had in with the other food.

She left the kitchen and walked the rest of the house to see what she could find. She had her personal pistol, issued by the Department of Homeland security, but anything else she could find would be a plus. She found a closet by the front door with some coats hanging in it and some shoes on the floor. Not what she was looking for so she closed the door. She found a second bedroom but it was a kid's bedroom. She didn't think there would be anything like what she was looking for in there so she didn't even try. She found a door that led to a basement. She went down the stairs and found a gun case in the corner. Its door was open so she went to look. A few of the rifles were missing but she did find a shotgun and a pistol. A large box was next to the gun case and she looked inside of it. The entire box was full of ammunition. Jenna put the pistol in her belt, slung the shotgun over her right shoulder, and bent low to grab the box. She grabbed the box and stood. She walked back up the stairs and made her way to the master bedroom. Jenna quietly set down the box of ammo at the foot of the bed and set both the shotgun and pistol on top of the box. She walked over to the bedroom door, shut it, and then locked it. She then pulled out her personal pistol and walked to the opposite side of the bed from where Colton was sleeping. She slipped off her shoes but kept her clothes on. Jenna slid into the bed, on top of all of the sheets and covers, and laid silently. With her hand wrapped around her pistol, she placed it on her chest. She closed her eyes and hoped sleep would come.

33

Jenna awoke with a start. A dog was barking outside. She opened her eyes and let the light, which was seeping in through the window, fill them. She realized that she still had her hand wrapped tightly around her pistol. She let go of it and her hand hurt. Jenna pumped her fist to try to get the blood to start flowing again. She looked over at Colton and he was staring at her. She started and almost fell out of the bed.

"You bastard," she said to Colton and lightly hit him on the shoulder.

Colton laughed and said, "You look cute when you sleep."

She smiled and said, "Come on, let's get some food."

As she was getting out of the bed, Jenna asked Colton, "How do you feel?"

He looked at her and said, "Well, I feel okay. It might take me another day to get back my energy but some food would help that go a long way. I actually think I can get out of the bed on my own."

Colton swung his feet over the side and slowly dropped to the floor. Jenna was there to support him and he grabbed onto her arm.

"You just wanted to touch me," she said.

He smiled and said, "Maybe."

Jenna let go of him and Colton stood fine. She walked with him to the kitchen and he sat down at the table. Jenna went to the fridge and shuffled through it. She found a few things and brought them out.

"Okay so the power is still on here," said Jenna. "But I think we should be careful with what we do. Cooking should be fine but no lights."

"I don't get it," said Colton. "Why do we have to be careful? Isn't the world dead outside?"

"Yes, but there are still people like you and me. And with those people, there is still chaos happening. It's lawless out there. Granted, not everyone is like that but we have to be careful."

"Okay," Colton said without argument.

Jenna found what she needed in the kitchen to make themselves something to eat. She finished and they sat at the table talking about what was going on.

'The thing is," Jenna said, "I don't even know why you and I never got sick. I took a big risk coming to see if I could get you out of the CDC. For that matter, I don't understand why there are still so many people alive out there." Colton reached into his pocket and handed Boone's note to Jenna.

"This is what I grabbed from Boone's hand when we were leaving the CDC," said Colton. Jenna read it out loud.

"There is no cure. O- is the key to staying alive. What?"

"Boone talked to me before he disappeared to do more work on this virus outbreak. He said he had found out why people like us were not being affected by the virus. It had to do with our blood type, O-. He hypothesized that O- either did not allow the virus to continue to live or it did not facilitate its transfer throughout the body. It was something like that. I'm not a biologist."

Jenna just stared at him. "This can't be happening," she said.

"Well, it is," said Colton. "I do have an idea though. I think we should get with others that are like us. I don't just mean survivors but survivors that act like us. I think if we band together we can make a better stand at surviving."

"Ok…" stammered Jenna looking for Colton to continue.

"I know a couple that should have survived the virus," said Colton.

Jenna stared at him for a moment. Then the lightbulb went off in her head.

"It's the Taylor's isn't it?" she asked.

Colton just took a bite of his food and nodded.

"Yeah as long as something or someone else hasn't gotten to them yet," said Jenna.

"We'll be fine," said Colton. "Let's finish eating and rest up today." Colton turned and opened the fridge.

"It looks like with what you grabbed at the CDC and what is in here we should be fine for a few days." He shut the fridge and turned back around to Jenna.

"Normally it wouldn't take maybe between eight to nine hours to get where we are going. But with what the outside world is, well, I just can't tell you how long it will take. We need as many supplies as we can get our hands on just in case we get stuck somewhere. We'll take everything from here and we can try to stop at places along the way. There may be others like us out there but that number is a small one compared to the previous population of the world. We should have no trouble findings things."

"Which reminds me…" said Jenna out loud. "Follow me."

They both stood up from the table, Colton a little slower than Jenna, and went back to the bedroom. Jenna bent down at the end of the bed and grabbed the ammo box with the guns on top. She set it on the bed and Colton came over.

"I found these in the basement. Figured they might come in handy."

Colton grabbed the shotgun and looked it over. "Mossberg 500. Nice gun. How many shells we have in that box?"

Jenna opened the box and they both looked in. There were three boxes of twenty-five. All three boxes were slug rounds. The rest of the box was filled with 9mm shells for the pistol.

"We'll obviously take it all," said Colton. "But let's load up as much as we can now so we are prepared when we leave. I'll start with the shotgun if you want to start with the pistol. Load up your personal pistol as well. Are there any extra magazines in there?"

Jenna shuffled the ammo around and came out with three extra magazines for the pistol.

"Those extra mags are a different size than the one you are carrying," said Colton. "Let's do this. Load up those magazines and then you can take that pistol and the extra mags. I'll ensure your personal pistol is loaded up and then I will take it and the shotgun. Sound good?"

"Sounds good to me," said Jenna. "After we do this let's go back to bed. As you said we are going to need our rest. We don't have to sleep but we need to rest. Tomorrow morning we will load everything up and get it in the car. Then we will head out."

"I like it. We may have to upgrade your car somewhere along the way. We'll see."

Both Colton and Jenna started loading the guns together.

34

Over the next day, both Jenna and Colton slept as much as they could. Rest would be very important, especially for Colton. When lunch and dinner time came around Jenna helped Colton to the table and she fixed them something to eat. Colton was getting better at getting around and so by the end of the night, Jenna let him do things on his own. They continued to search the house for items that they might need for their upcoming travel. They found a few things here and there and they hoped that on the drive up to Indiana that they would be able to get more. Colton was confident they would.

They had found some candles on one of their searches through the house and decided they would use them once darkness fell. They found some clothes in the master bedroom and tried them on. The female's clothes that were in the closet were a little too big for Jenna but they would do. She took several pairs of jeans and shirts out of the closet and started to match them up. Colton found that the male's clothes in the closet were not his taste. Rock t-shirts, as well as "one-liner" t-shirts, were abundant. Even though they were not his taste he grabbed them anyway. He knew he may need something more in the days to come. The jeans were too small in the closet and so Colton would have to settle for what he had on in the meantime.

Before they were done gathering clothes they noticed that the sun had started to set. Jenna went to grab the candles and a few matches while Colton started to shut the blinds and curtains throughout the house. They had left the lights off in the house for a reason so there was no need for anyone to see the light coming from the candles. Soon they were back to grabbing and folding clothes by candlelight. They had found a medium-sized suitcase in the closet and they were packing all of the clothing in there. They could easily throw it in the back of the car and be done with it.

They had found two backpacks in the kid's room and decided they would take both of them. They could come in handy if they needed to hike or walk for any reason. They decided to pack one set of clothes in the backpacks and when they woke up in the morning some food would also go into each one. For the rest of the food, they had found a clothes basket and they could stack everything in there and then put it in the back seat of the car. Other than the clothes, guns, food, and packs, they decided there wasn't much else that they wanted to take. Sure, there could be an argument for a lot of things but there was a big line between *need* and *want*. Okay so maybe they could take the candles and matches with them. They had to be careful with starting a fire but it could also be a good thing.

When bedtime came around, neither of them were really tired as they had tried to rest all day. However, knowing they would need it, and not knowing if they would miss out on rest in the next few days, they settled into sleep. Jenna had blown out all of the candles but one. That one candle sat on her side of the bed. They both slid into the bed and slid under the covers. They had found a few sets of shorts and t-shirts that they were willing to wear as pajamas. They laid next to each other and talked for a while. Both wondering what was going to happen next. Both wondering what had happened to friends and family. Both suddenly wondering what was happening between the two of them. They smiled at each other and slid closer together. Jenna leaned over and blew out the candle. Complete darkness enveloped them and they hugged each other tighter. They soon fell asleep holding each other.

As the sun rose over the houses and trees a few slivers found their way through the blinds and poked at both Jenna and Colton. They stirred and realized that today was the day they were leaving. They both rose from the bed and stretched. Colton felt better today and he was the first one out of the bed. He also beat Jenna to the kitchen and made them a quick breakfast. Afterward, they packed everything up and put it in the car. They kept hold of the guns until they were ready to leave. With the clothes, ammo, and food packed in the car, they were ready to go. Colton reached in and started the car. Jenna sat shotgun and Colton moved over to hit the garage door opener on the garage wall. The door started to slide open and Colton jumped in the running car. As soon as the door was open Colton put the car in reverse and backed out.

They hit the street and Colton put the car into drive. He started driving north looking for the main road that would take them to the highway.

"Can you get the GPS working?" asked Colton.

"Oh yeah," said Jenna. She reached into her center console and brought out a GPS unit.

"Do you remember the address?" asked Jenna.

"No, but, just get us to the city and I think I could remember how to get there."

"You were only there once, are you sure?"

Colton tapped the side of his head and smiled.

"It's all in here," he said.

Jenna guffawed and shook her head.

———————————◆———————————

They had only been driving for a few hours when they stopped. Colton had pulled into a car dealership. He was looking for a 4x4 truck that they could take the rest of the way. It might be hell on gas mileage but it would help them get through almost anything plus it had more room that Jenna's car. They were still looking for supplies as they continued on. They were able to get into the dealership's office where all the keys were, breaking and entering didn't exist anymore, and they found a set of keys to a large truck out in the lot. They changed their supplies from the car to the truck. As they were about to leave they heard gunshots. They jumped in quickly and sped off. Colton attempted to drive the truck in the opposite direction of the gunfire. He succeeded but then had the truck going in the opposite direction they were supposed to be heading. The GPS soon spoke up and took them back to the highway they had been traveling on.

Often times Colton had to swerve for traffic. Not moving traffic mind you but plenty of abandoned cars. It seemed the sick just didn't make it home or to the hospital. Plenty of people died right where they were whether that was on the street in their car or just collapsing on the sidewalk. Plenty of dead bodies were around and Colton and Jenna tried to avoid them as much as possible. Twice they had to pull off of the highway for gas. Colton pumped while Jenna looked for more supplies. Surprisingly the power was still on at the pumps. Colton knew it would go soon with no one running the power plants, but for now, he was grateful. Jenna had found food supplies to last awhile but many items were expendable and would go bad soon. They took them anyway.

On both gas and supply breaks they noticed many houses that had red X's on the front doors. Looking around there were plenty of red Xs so Colton didn't think that the X's had helped the residents within the communities. They caught sight of several small groups as well as individual people while they were driving. Either those people did not care to follow or they did not see Colton and Jenna. The latter was hard to believe so Colton hoped that they had better things to do than to follow, namely surviving. It wasn't too long out of Georgia that Colton had to engage the 4x4. He slowed down and turned on his wipers. They had hit the Appalachian Mountains and it would be slow going for a while. Soon they would head west on the highway and they would leave the mountains.

After having to slow down considerable just to stay on the road they decided to stop at a rest stop along the highway. They ate a little bit and because the 4x4 truck they had borrowed was a Hummer, there was enough room in the back for them to lie down. They made sure the doors were locked and they went to sleep. As dawn neared Colton woke up shivering. He was physically shaking from the cold and he decided to turn on the truck to get some heat. He climbed to the front of the truck and started it. Colton noticed that outside the snow had stopped. He decided he was going to drive on while Jenna slept. She would probably be awake soon anyhow but it would be best to get moving early. He put the truck in drive and pulled out of the rest stop. He did not take the truck out of four-wheel drive before they went to bed and so when he hit big patches of snow and ice coming out of the rest stop he was thankful they had changed vehicles.

After about an hour of driving, Jenna stirred. Colton was surprised the bumpy roads and general movement of the vehicle had not woken her until now. She yawned, stretched, and then climbed into the front of the truck.

"Did you sleep okay," asked Colton.

"Define okay," grumbled Jenna.

Colton chortled and nodded in understanding. His back hurt as well from the hard placemat in the back of the Hummer. Jenna lightly grasped his arm and let go.

"How about I find us something to nibble on," stated Jenna.

"That would be nice," responded Colton. "My stomach has growled so many times I thought it was eating itself."

Jenna eyed him with a suspicious look and then made her way back to the back of the truck. She shuffled a few things around and then came up with some fruit they had gotten from the kitchen of the house they had stayed at. She split it up evenly and handed some to Colton. They both ate it voraciously.

Several hours later they stopped to stretch their legs. Colton pulled over to the side of the road and put the truck in park.

"Stay here for a minute," he said to Jenna.

He waited for her to acknowledge and then he jumped out. He quickly looked around trying to lay eyes on anything that could be a threat. It was a long stretch of highway and Colton felt like he could see forever down it. The only thing in the vicinity of where he parked was either abandoned cars or cars that had people in them that could not escape the virus. These cars were scattered along the highway but not bad enough that Colton and Jenna could not get through. There was a forest off to the right but it was far enough back that if someone was hiding in anticipation of other cars, they would see them come out.

Colton motioned for Jenna to come out. She stepped out and instantly went into a stretch.

"It feels so good to get out and stretch," she said.

"How about while you do that I find something we can eat. It'll be small, since now is not the time to cook anything, but I know we have something in there."

Jenna nodded and continued stretching. Colton dug into the food until he found something. He passed it to her and they ate. He got a few stretches in and then decided it was time to move on.

"Wanna drive?" Colton asked.

"Of course," said Jenna. They both smiled and then traded places in the truck. Once they hopped in Colton reached over and turned off the four-wheel drive. The roads had gotten a lot better and they would not need it anymore.

"I know how to drive," said Jenna.

"Just helping out," said Colton as he stuck his hands in the air and slinked back over to his side of the truck.

"Well, if I need help I'll ask," said Jenna as she leaned over to his side of the truck. Colton leaned in towards her as well and they met in the middle. They kissed each other and held that embrace for a moment. Jenna pulled away first.

"Let's get going!" she hollered.

They both gave a little whoop as Jenna started the truck, put it into drive, and slammed on the gas.

It was nearing early evening when they pulled into the neighborhood where the Taylors lived. As they drove along, each house they passed had a red X on it. It seemed humanity had seen enough movies to know that a red X is bad, and by putting one on your door it let people know to stay out. Colton wondered if people really stayed out. Jenna pulled up to the Taylor's house, by direction of Colton, and put the truck in park. They were still parked in the street and were scared of what they would find. The Taylor's house also had a red X on the door.

"Maybe they just did that to scare people off," said Colton. "That's what I would do."

"But what if they caught the virus and are dead. Then we just wasted a trip up here," said Jenna.

"I don't think they are dead. Remember what I said about blood types being the key. Dr. Boone said that when he tested their blood that it was O-. They have to be alive," responded Colton.

Jenna looked at him. "Well, there is only one way to find out." Jenna put the truck into drive and pulled into the driveway. They got out together and looked around the neighborhood. It was quiet and Colton saw no one. Someone could be hiding and if so they needed to be careful. Colton walked around the truck and over to Jenna.

"Ready?" he asked.

"Let's do this," whispered Jenna.

They both walked up to the front door together. They rapped softly on the door and waited. No one came to the door.

"Maybe…" started Jenna. At that moment Colton could have sworn that he saw the front curtains move slightly.

"Someone is in there," he said. Colton got a little closer to the door and knocked again. This time he followed up the knock with his voice.

"Mr. and Mrs. Taylor. It's Agent Colton Johns with Homeland Security. Do you remember me? Please if you are in there let us in. We are survivors like you. We have information and want to talk. Please."

It was silent for a minute and then Colton heard the door unlock. Before he could do anything a 9mm was stuffed firmly in his face. Colton froze immediately but was able to get a few words out.

"It's me," was all he said. The gun slowly dropped and Donald looked past both of them and eyed his neighborhood.

"You have answers?" asked Donald.

"Yes we do," said Colton.

"Who is this?" asked Donald pointing to Jenna.

"This is Jenna Walsh. She also works for Homeland Security. Can we come in?"

Donald looked around one more time and said, "I guess there's not much homeland to secure anymore, is there? I'll get the garage door. One of you pull the truck in. The other one come in and make yourself comfortable."

With a smile and a nod, both Jenna and Colton felt like things were going to change.

35

2 DAYS EARLIER...

Sanjar Ahmadi lay in his bed at home feeling horrible. He had developed a cough and then blood started to come out of orifices where it shouldn't come out. His wife had laid him down in bed and then she catered to him trying to get him well. The boils and sores soon followed and Sanjar did not know how it had happened. He thought he had had control over the virus and its alterations. Somehow other strains had been released and the whole world was dying. He tried to stay away from almost everyone but somehow he still caught the virus. His feet and legs were in horrific pain and he hadn't gotten out of bed for the last twelve hours.

It wasn't long until his hands were sore enough that he couldn't even hold the cup that his wife had brought him. Sanjar's wife attempted to keep his face clean but the blood and pus were constantly accumulating and running down his neck. She eventually gave up when she, too, started feeling ill. Soon his eyesight gave out and he knew that his time was nigh. *Well, at least I'll get to be with my 72 virgins,* thought Sanjar. When his eyes closed, they did not open again. He experienced nothing but darkness and death.